WHISPERING IN THE DARK

Ruskin Bond is known for his signature simplistic and witty writing style. He is the author of several bestselling short stories, novellas, collections, essays and children's books; and has contributed a number of poems and articles to various magazines and anthologies. At the age of twenty-three, he won the prestigious John Llewellyn Rhys Prize for his first novel, *The Room on the Roof*. He was also the recipient of the Padma Shri in 1999, Lifetime Achievement Award by the Delhi Government in 2012, and the Padma Bhushan in 2014.

Born in 1934, Ruskin Bond grew up in Jamnagar, Shimla, New Delhi and Dehradun. Apart from three years in the UK, he has spent all his life in India, and now lives in Landour, Mussoorie, with his adopted family.

WHISPERING IN THE DARK

Edited & Compiled by

RUSKIN BOND

RUPA

Published by
Rupa Publications India Pvt. Ltd 2018
7/16, Ansari Road, Daryaganj
New Delhi 110002

Sales centres:
Allahabad Bengaluru Chennai
Hyderabad Jaipur Kathmandu
Kolkata Mumbai

ISBN: 978-93-5304-127-4

First impression 2018

10 9 8 7 6 5 4 3 2 1

CONTENTS

INTRODUCTION

When I run out of relatives, I invent ghosts. I don't find the two very different. As a child, when I lived with my grandmother, my many aunts and Uncle Ken would visit us rather often. In those days, I much preferred settling down with the ghosts of my creation for a cosy night or assisting Dukhi, our gardener, in plotting ways to mess with my stepfather.

A great imagination makes for terrific ghost stories. I personally like the ones that go beyond the tapping on doors in the middle of the night or a sinister wailing of the wind. And that is why I have put together this collection of horror stories that will do more than just send shivers down your spine when you read it.

E. and H. Heron, an original pair, combined the supernatural with 'psychological detection'. In psychologist Flaxman Low they created the Sherlock Holmes of the ghost story. He is at his best in 'The Story of the Spaniards, Hammersmith'.

There is Algernon Blackwood's 'The Decoy'. Blackwood could take suspense and horror to almost unbearable lengths. He had few peers in the realm of the supernatural. His 'The Empty House' is a classic story of this kind—the narrator's aunt summons him to come and explore the empty house with her. It looks like every other house on that street but has a dreadful past and holds its secrets close. As soon as they enter the house, they know that something or someone is watching them. Someone who was clearly not looking forward to their arrival.

Perceval Landon's 'Thurnley Abbey', where a supposedly friendly hoax turns out to be the real thing will scare you out of your wits. Alice Perrin, the wife of a British official, spent many years in India. She was an accomplished novelist and short-story writer. Her jungle thriller, 'The White Tiger', will certainly thrill you. Arthur Morrison was another fine writer and he went around the poorer parts of London and Paris to research for his haunting tales like 'The Thing in the Upper Room'.

Rudyard Kipling wrote a number of successful ghost stories, most of which were set in India. I first heard the story of 'The Phantom 'Rickshaw' from my father, when he took me to Shimla for my boarding school admission. During the mid-term break, he took me for a rickshaw ride around the town and on the way he recounted Kipling's story, which still seems real to me.

These and many more such stories by writers such as Ambrose Bierce, Lady Eleanor Smith, Sydney Horler, John Eyton, among others together form this collection of tales of horror set in India as well as in other countries. As you flee from your bedroom to escape their ghostly presence, you will find them waiting for you at the bottom of the stairs. The night has a thousand eyes, and the day but one!

Ruskin Bond

ONE SUMMER NIGHT

Ambrose Bierce

The fact that Henry Armstrong was buried did not seem to him to prove that he was dead; he had always been a hard man to convince. That he really was buried, the testimony of his senses compelled him to admit. His posture—flat upon his back, with hands crossed upon his stomach and tied with something that he easily broke without profitably altering the situation—the strict confinement of his entire person, the black darkness and profound silence, made a body of evidence impossible to controvert and he accepted it without cavil.

But dead—no; he was only very, very ill. He had, withal, the invalid's apathy and did not greatly concern himself about the uncommon fate that had been allotted to him. No philosopher was he—just a plain, commonplace person gifted, for the time being, with a pathological indifference: the organ that he feared consequences with was torpid. So, with no particular apprehension for his immediate future, he fell asleep and all was peace with Henry Armstrong.

But something was going on overhead. It was a dark summer night, shot through with infrequent shimmers of lightning silently firing a cloud lying low in the west and portending a storm.

These brief, stammering illuminations brought out with ghastly distinctness the monuments and headstones of the cemetery and seemed to set them dancing. It was not a night in which any credible witness was likely to be straying about a cemetery, so the three men who were there, digging into the grave of Henry Armstrong, felt reasonably secure.

Two of them were young students from a medical college a few miles away; the third was a gigantic man known as Jess. For many years Jess had been employed about the cemetery as a man-of-all-work and it was his favourite pleasantry that he knew 'every soul in the place.' From the nature of what he was now doing it was inferable that the place was not so populous as its register may have shown it to be.

Outside the wall, at the part of the grounds furthest from the public road, were a horse and a light wagon, waiting.

The work of excavation was not difficult: the earth with which the grave had been loosely filled a few hours before offered little resistance and was soon thrown out. Removal of the casket from its box was less easy, but it was taken out, for it was a perquisite of Jess, who carefully unscrewed the cover and laid it aside, exposing the body in black trousers and white shirt. At that instant the air sprang to flame, a cracking shock of thunder shook the stunned world, and Henry Armstrong tranquilly sat up. With inarticulate cries the men fled in terror, each in a different direction. For nothing on earth could two of them have been persuaded to return. But Jess was of another breed.

In the grey of the morning the two students, pallid and haggard from anxiety and with the terror of their adventure still beating tumultuously in their blood, met at the medical college.

'You saw it?' cried one.

'God! Yes—what are we to do?' They went around to the rear of the building, where they saw a horse, attached to a light wagon, hitched to a gatepost near the door of the dissecting-room. Mechanically they entered the room. On a bench in the obscurity sat Jess. He rose, grinning, all eyes and teeth. 'I'm waiting for my pay,' he said. Stretched naked on a long table lay the body of Henry Armstrong, the head defiled with blood and clay from a blow with a spade.

DEATH IN THE KITCHEN

Milward Kennedy

Rupert Morrison straightened himself, drawing a deep breath. He glanced round the little kitchen, deliberately looking at the figure which lay huddled on the floor; huddled, but yet in an attitude which Morrison hoped was as natural as its unnatural circumstances would permit. For the head was inside the oven of the rusty-looking gas-stove.

He wondered whether the cushion on which the head rested was a natural or an unnatural touch. He decided that if he were committing suicide, he would try to make even a gas-oven as comfortable as possible.

He walked silently (for he was in stockinged feet) into the passage, and so to the sitting-room. The curtains he had drawn so carefully that he had had no hesitation in leaving on the lights. Quickly but methodically he set to work. Nothing must be left which connected him in any way with George Manning. In any way? Well, how about that package addressed not to Manning but to himself from the local grocer? Probably it had been delivered in error. Still, he must take no chances. He put it aside for future attention.

Where did Manning keep his papers? He was a careless devil, not likely to hide them securely or ingeniously. No, here they were in the writing-table. Only six that concerned Rupert Morrison; was that really all? He untied the packet and read each of the six. His cheeks reddened as he read; they were certainly damning. What a fool he had been in those days: still, he had been wise enough to remember it when Manning turned up out of the blue (he could not have spent all the interval in gaol?) and started his blackmail. George Manning on the other hand had grown foolish, for he had not troubled to discover whether his victim had changed.

Morrison's clumsy gloved hands thrust the packet into his breast pocket. He considered. He had plenty of time. Manning, he knew, lived alone in the cottage, and had few friends, certainly none who were likely to call on him; his domestic staff was limited to an old woman from the distant village who came in for part of the day.

The important thing was to be thorough. He had no alibi, and knew that it would be folly to fake one. Provided that there was nothing to show that he had a motive for wanting Manning dead, he would not have to account for his own whereabouts; his tale of a country tramp across the fields and through the woods would not even be wanted. Outside the cottage there was, he knew, nothing to suggest any relationship between Manning and himself save such as might exist between two men, friends long ago in schooldays, who had drifted apart, and then by chance met again: the one respected and prosperous, the other—George Manning.

At last he was satisfied with the sitting-room, but there were still the two bedrooms. Bare shabby rooms they were, and they did not keep him long. Down to the 'parlour' once more. He was reluctant to leave it, for there, if anywhere, he would leave behind a key to the truth.

But he could think of nothing more, except the tumblers on the table and the grocer's package.

There must be only one glass, of course; one must be washed and put away in the kitchen. The other? It, too, must be washed, for when it was found there must be no trace of anything more deadly in it than whisky. Of course, he could wash it and provide fresh prints of Manning's fingers.

He had to make two journeys to the kitchen with the 'properties' for the scene which he must set.

Soon one tumbler was back in the cupboard; the other, on which, after he had washed it, he had carefully pressed Manning's limp hand, stood on the table, a trace of neat whisky in it. Beside it the bottle, nearly empty; Manning certainly had been putting it away. That, no doubt, was why he had been so unnoticing when Morrison (none too neatly) had emptied his little flask into the tumbler. He gave a worried glance at the body; if the dose had been too strong the whole plan might go astray. But that was absurd—he had felt the pulse only a minute ago.

And now the last detail—to put that half-sheet of paper on the table. He placed it to look as if it had been folded to catch the eye; he dared not forge a superscription to the coroner.

He smiled; it was a bit of luck that those words so exactly filled a half-sheet in Manning's letter. Directly he had received it, months ago, he had seen its possible value.

'I am tired of it all. Who can blame me for taking the easiest way? So take it smiling—as I propose to do.—GEORGE MANNING.' But it was cash that Manning had meant to take with a smile—not coal-gas.

There. And the window tight shut. Now to turn on the gas, leave the electric light burning, and be gone. Footprints? No, his stockinged feet had left none, he was sure. Boots on. Quietly out by the back door, with nothing to carry but a walking stick and that grocer's packet...

Not a soul did Morrison meet on his way home, and when he had emptied the packet of sugar down the wash basin, and in the same way disposed of the ashes of its cover and of those six letters he took another deep breath—of relief this time... Naturally the police would come to him, for he was a man of standing and he was known to be on terms of acquaintance with Manning. He would be able to tell them that the 'poor chap' had seemed very neurotic... His 'Good morning' smile as the sergeant was shown in at these thoughts as well as a matter of policy.

'Yes, sergeant, I know him slightly.' By Jove! As nearly as no matter he had said 'knew'; he must watch his tongue.

'D'you recognise this, sir?'

Good God! What was the man holding up? A pocketbook, dark blue, with a monogram. He put his hand to his breast pocket. No—could he. He had an appalling memory of pushing those papers into his pocket. His gloved fingers had felt so clumsy. *Could* he have pulled it out and left it lying on the carpet—there?

He put out his hand; his power of speech seemed to have vanished. He took the pocketbook, half surprised that the sergeant allowed him to do so, and turned it over and over, and stared at it. What use was a denial?

The sergeant was speaking. Was he warning him that anything he might say...?

'That's the boy from Bayley's, the grocer, sir. Seems he

delivered the wrong parcel—one for you, it was. Left it last evening at the cottage. Went first thing to get it back. Couldn't get a reply and the front door was locked, so he went round to the back. It seems the back door was open—of course, sir, he hadn't no right to go in, but...'

Why *would* the fool bother about that? Go on, man. My heart won't stand this.

'Electric light burning in the kitchen and this Manning lying with his head inside the oven. Gave the boy a shock, so he says, but if you ask me... Anyways, he came along on his bike to me—I found the pocketbook, sir, in the sitting-room. I thought I'd have a word with you. You see, this Mr Manning—well—sir, there's a police record.'

Why must he pause? Did he expect an answer? Morrison could only stare, his lips trembling.

'Course, sir. You may have given it to him. Or it may just have been an accident...'

What was 'it'? Even if he could have spoken, Morrison would have refused now.

'But apart from that, sir—his record and that, I mean—it struck me there was something queer about Manning. And I thought maybe you could help me. That gas-oven, sir, that looks like suicide, doesn't it, sir?'

'Yes—I suppose so.'

Was that really his voice?

'There was a bottle of whisky on the table—that came from Baylcy's yesterday afternoon, too, and it was empty all but a drain this morning. Maybe it was that that did it...'

What *had* gone wrong? How had this local bumpkin stumbled on the truth?

'At any rate, sir, whisky or lunacy, would you have thought

anyone, drunk or sober, could put his head in a gas-oven and turn the tap—and forget the gas was cut off because he hadn't paid the bill? I can understand how it is; he's forgotten every blamed thing about what happened last night, but—Hallo, sir, what's up?'

Rupert Morrison was lying at the sergeant's feet.

THE DEAD MAN OF VARLEY GRANGE

A Victorian Ghost Story by Anonymous

'Hallo, Jack! Where are you off to? Going down to the governor's place for Christmas?'

Jack Darent, who was in my old regiment, stood drawing on his dogskin gloves upon 23 December the year before last. He was equipped in a long Ulster and top hat, and a hansom, already loaded with a gun-case and portmanteau, stood awaiting him. He had a tall, strong figure, a fair, fresh-looking face, and the merriest blue eyes in the world. He held cigarette between his lips, and late as was the season of the year there was a flower in his buttonhole. When did I ever see handsome Jack Darent and he did not look well dressed and well fed and jaunty? As I ran up the steps of the Club he turned round and laughed merrily.

'My dear fellow, do I look the sort of man to be victimized at a family Christmas meeting? Do you know the kind of business they have at home? Three maiden aunts and a bachelor uncle, my eldest brother and his insipid wife, and all my sister's six noisy children at dinner. Church twice a day, and snap-dragon between the services! No, thank you! I have a great affection for my old patents, but you don't catch me going in for that sort of national festival!'

'You irreverent ruffian!' I replied, laughing. 'Ah, if you were a married man—'

'Ah, if I were a married man!' replied Captain Darent with something that was almost a sigh, and then, lowering his voice, he said hurriedly, 'How is Miss Lester, Fred?'

'My sister is quite well, thank you,' I answered with becoming gravity; and it was not without spice of malice that I added, 'She has been going out to a great many halls and enjoying herself very much.'

Captain Darent looked profoundly miserable.

'I don't see how a poor fellow in a marching regiment, a younger son too, with nothing in the future to look to, is ever to marry nowadays,' he said almost savagely; 'When girls, too, are used to so much luxury and extravagance that they can't live without it. Matrimony is at a deadlock in this century, Fred, chiefly owing to the price of butchers' meat and bonnets. In fifty years' time it will become extinct and the country be depopulated. But I must be off, old man, or I shall miss my train.'

'You have never told me where you are going to, Jack.'

'Oh, I am going to stay with old Henderson in Westernshire; he has taken a furnished house with some first-rate pheasant shooting for a year. There are seven of us going—all bachelors, and all kindred spirits. We shall shoot all day and smoke half the night. Think what you have lost, old fellow, by becoming a Benedick!'

'In Westernshire, is it?' I inquired. 'Whereabouts is this place, and what is the name of it? For I am a Westernshire man by birth myself, and I know every place in the county.'

'Oh, it's a tumbledown sort of old house, I believe,'

answered Jack carelessly. 'Gables and twisted chimneys outside, and uncomfortable spindle-legged furniture inside—you know the sort of thing; but the shooting is capital, Henderson says, and we must put up with our quarters. He has taken his French cook down, and plenty of liquor, so I've no doubt we shan't starve.'

'Well, but what is the name of it?' I persisted, with a growing interest in the subject.

'Let me see,' referring to a letter he pulled out of his pocket. 'Oh, here it is—Varley Grange.'

'Varley Grange!' I repeated, aghast. 'Why, it has not been inhabited for years.'

'I believe not,' answered Jack unconcernedly. 'The shooting has been let separately; but Henderson took a fancy to the house too and thought it would do for him, furniture and all, just as it is. My dear Fred, what are you looking so solemnly at me for?'

'Jack, let me entreat of you not to go to this place,' I said, laying my hand on his arm.

'Not go! Why, Lester, you must be mad! Why on earth shouldn't I go there?'

'There are stories—uncomfortable things said of that house.' I had not the moral courage to say, 'It is haunted,' and I felt myself how weak and childish was my attempt to deter him from his intended visit; only—I knew all about Varley Grange.

I think handsome Jack Darent thought privately that I was slightly out of my senses, for I am sure I looked unaccountably upset and dismayed by the mention of the name of the house that Mr Henderson had taken.

'I daresay it's cold and draughty and infested with rats and mice,' he said laughingly; 'and I have no doubt the creature-comforts will not be equal to Queen's Gate; but I stand pledged to go now, and I must be off this very minute, so have no time, old fellow, to inquire into the meaning of your sensational warning. Goodbye, and—and remember me to the ladies.'

He ran down the steps and jumped into the hansom.

'Write to me if you have time!' I cried out after him; but I don't think he heard me in the rattle of the departing cab. He nodded and smiled at me and was swiftly whirled out of sight.

As for me, I walked slowly back to my comfortable house in Queen's Gate. There was my wife presiding at the little five o'clock tea-table, our two fat, pink and white little children tumbling about upon the hearthrug amongst dolls and bricks, and two utterly spoilt and overfed pugs; and my sister Bella— who, between ourselves, was the prettiest as well as dearest girl in all London—sitting on the floor in her handsome brown velvet gown, resigning herself gracefully to be trampled upon by the dogs, and to have her hair pulled by the babies.

'Why, Fred, you look as if you had heard bad news,' said my wife, looking up anxiously as I entered.

'I don't know that I have heard of anything very bad; I have just seen Jack Darent off for Christmas,' I said, turning instinctively towards my sister. He was a poor man and a younger son, and of course a very bad match for the beautiful Miss Lester; but for all that I had an inkling that Bella was not quite indifferent to her brother's friend.

'Oh!' says that hypocrite. 'Shall I give you a cup of tea, Fred?'

It is wonderful how women can control their faces and pretend not to care a straw when they hear the name of their lover mentioned. I think Bella overdid it, she looked so supremely indifferent.

'Where on earth do you suppose he is going to stay, Bella?'

'Who? Oh, Captain Darent! How should I possibly know where he is going? Archie, pet, please don't poke the doll's head quite down Ponto's throat; I know he will bite it off if you do.'

This last observation was addressed to my son and heir.

'Well, I think you will be surprised when you hear: he is going to Westernshire, to stay at Varley Grange.'

'*What!*' No doubt about her interest in the subject now! Miss Lester turned as white as her collar and sprang to her feet impetuously, scattering dogs, babies and toys in all directions away from her skirts as she rose.

'You cannot mean it, Fred! Varley Grange, why, it has not been inhabited for ten years; and the last time—Oh, do you remember those poor people who took it? What a terrible story it has!' She shuddered.

'Well, it is taken now,' I said, 'by a man I know, called Henderson—a bachelor; he has asked down a party of men for a week's shooting, and Jack Darent is one of them.'

'For Heaven's sake prevent him from going!' cried Bella, clasping her hands.

'My dear, he is gone!'

'Oh, then write to him—telegraph—tell him to come back!' she urged breathlessly.

'I am afraid it is no use,' I said gravely 'He would not come back; he would not believe me; he would think I was mad.'

'Did you tell him anything?' she asked faintly.

'No, I had no time. I did say a word or two, but he began to laugh.'

'Yes, that is how it always is!' she said distractedly. 'People laugh and pooh-pooh the whole thing, and then they go there and see for themselves, and it is too late!'

She was so thoroughly upset that she left the room. My wife turned to me in astonishment; not being a Westernshire woman, she was not well up in the traditions of that venerable county.

'What on earth does it all mean, Fred?' she asked me in amazement. 'What is the matter with Bella, and why is she so distressed that Captain Darent is going to stay at that particular house?'

'It is said to be haunted, and—'

'You don't mean to say you believe in such rubbish, Fred?' interrupted my wife sternly, with a side-glance of apprehension at our first-born who, needless to say, stood by, all eyes and ears, drinking in every word of the conversation of his elders.

'I never know what I believe or what I don't believe,' I answered gravely, 'All I can say is that there are very singular traditions about that house, and that a great many credible witnesses have seen a very strange thing there, and that a great many disasters have happened to the persons who have seen it.'

'What has been seen, Fred? Pray tell me the story! Wait, I think I will send the children away.'

My wife rang the bell for the nurse, and as soon as the little ones had been taken from the room she turned to me again.

'I don't believe in ghosts or any such rubbish one bit, but I should like to hear your story.'

'The story is vague enough,' I answered.

'In the old days Varley Grange belonged to the ancient family of Varley, now completely extinct. There was, some hundred years ago, a daughter, famed for her beauty and her fascination. She wanted to marry a poor, penniless squire, who loved her devotedly. Her brother, Dennis Varley, the new owner of Varley Grange, refused his consent and shut his sister up in the nunnery that used to stand outside his park gates—there are a few ruins of it left still. The poor nun broke her vows and ran away in the night with her lover. But her brother pursued her and brought her back with him. The lover escaped, but the lord of Varley murdered his sister under his own roof, swearing that no scion of his race should live to disgrace and dishonour his ancient name.

'Ever since that day Dennis Varley's spirit cannot rest in its grave—he wanders about the old house at night time and those who have seen him are numberless. Now and then the pale, shadowy form of a nun flits across the old hall, or along the gloomy passages, and when both strange shapes are seen thus together misfortune and illness, and even death, is sure to pursue the luckless man who has seen them, with remorseless cruelty.'

'I wonder you believe in such rubbish,' says my wife at the conclusion of my tale.

I shrug my shoulders and answer nothing, for who are so obstinate as those who persist in disbelieving everything that they cannot understand?

◆

It was little more than a week later that, walking by myself along Pall Mall one afternoon, I suddenly came upon Jack Darent walking towards me.

'Hallo, Jack! Back again? Why, man, how odd you look!'

There was a change in the man that I was instantly aware of. His frank, careless face looked clouded and anxious, and the merry smile was missing from his handsome countenance.

'Come into the Club, Fred,' he said, taking me by the arm. 'I have something to say to you.'

He drew me into a corner of the Club's smoking-room.

'You were quite right. I wish to Heaven I had never gone to that house.'

'You mean—have you seen anything?' I inquired eagerly.

'I have seen *everything*,' he answered with a shudder. 'They say one dies within a year—'

'My dear fellow, don't be so upset about it,' I interrupted; I was quite distressed to see how thoroughly the man had altered.

'Let me tell you about it, Fred.'

He drew his chair close to mine and told me his story, pretty nearly in the following words:

'You remember the day I went down you had kept me talking at the Club door; I had a race to catch the train; however, I just did it. I found the other fellows all waiting for me. There was Charlie Wells, the two Harfords, Colonel Riddell, who is such a crack shot, two fellows in the Guards, both pretty fair, a man called Thompson, a barrister, Henderson and myself— eight of us in all. We had a remarkably lively journey down, as you may imagine, and reached Varley Grange in the highest possible spirits. We all slept like tops that night.

'The next day we were out from eleven till dusk among the coverts, and a better day's shooting I never enjoyed in the whole course of my life, the birds literally swarmed. We bagged a hundred and thirty brace. We were all pretty well tired when we got home, and did full justice to a very good dinner and first-class Perrier-Jouet. After dinner we adjourned to the hall to smoke. This hall is quite the feature of the house. It is large and bright, panelled halfway up with sombre old oak, and vaulted with heavy carved oaken rafters. At the farther end runs a gallery, into which opened the door of my bedroom, and shut off from the rest of the passages by a swing door at either end.

'Well, all we fellows sat up there smoking and drinking brandy and soda, and jawing, you know—as men always do when they are together—about sport of all kinds, hunting and shooting and salmon-fishing; and I assure you not one of us had a thought in our heads beyond relating some wonderful incident of a long shot or big fence by which he would each cap the last speaker's experiences. We were just, I recollect, listening to a long story of the old Colonel's, about his experiences among bisons in Cachemire, when suddenly one of us—I can't remember who it was—gave a sort of shout and started to his feet, pointing up to the gallery behind us. We all turned round, and there—I give you my word of honour, Lester—stood a man leaning over the rail of the gallery, staring down upon us.

'We all saw him. Every one of us. Eight of us, remember. He stood there full ten seconds, looking down with horrible glittering eyes at us. He had a long tawny beard, and his hands, that were crossed together before him, were nothing but skin and bone. But it was his face that was so unspeakably dreadful. It was livid—the face of a dead man!'

'How was he dressed?'

'I could not see; he wore some kind of a black cloak over his shoulders, I think, but the lower part of his figure was hidden behind the railings. Well, we all stood perfectly speechless for, as I said, about ten seconds; and then the figure moved, backing slowly into the door of the room behind him, which stood open. It was the door of my bedroom! As soon as he had disappeared our senses seemed to return to us. There was a general rush for the staircase, and, as you may imagine, there was not a corner of the house that was left unsearched; my bedroom especially was ransacked in every part of it. But all in vain; there was not the slightest trace to be found of any living being. You may suppose that not one of us slept that night. We lighted every candle and lamp we could lay hands upon and sat up till daylight, but nothing more was seen.

'The next morning, at breakfast, Henderson, who seemed very much annoyed by the whole thing, begged us not to speak of it any more. He said that he had been told, before he had taken the house, that it was supposed to be haunted; but, not being a believer in such childish follies, he had paid but little attention to the rumour. He did not, however, want it talked about, because of the servants, who would be so easily frightened. He was quite certain, he said, that the figure we had seen last night must be somebody dressed up to practise a trick upon us, and he recommended us all to bring our guns down loaded after dinner, but meanwhile to forget the startling apparition as far as we could.

'We, of course, readily agreed to do as he wished, although I do not think that one of us imagined for a moment that any amount of dressing-up would be able to simulate the awful countenance that we had all of us seen too plainly. It would have taken a Hare or an Arthur Cecil, with all the theatrical appliances known only to those two talented actors, to have 'made-up' the face, that was literally that of a corpse. Such a person could not be amongst us—actually in the house— without our knowledge.

'We had another good day's shooting, and by degrees the fresh air and exercise and the excitement of the sport obliterated the impression of what we had seen in some measure from the minds of most of us. That evening we all appeared in the hall after dinner with our loaded guns besides us; but, although we sat up till the small hours and looked frequently up at the gallery at the end of the hall, nothing at all disturbed us that night.

'Two nights thus went by and nothing further was seen of the gentleman with the tawny beard. What with the good company, the good cheer and the pheasants, we had pretty well forgotten all about him.

'We were sitting as usual upon the third night, with our

pipes and our cigars; a pleasant glow from the bright wood fire in the great chimney lighted up the old hall, and shed a genial warmth about us; when suddenly it seemed to me as if there came a breath of cold, chill air behind me, such as one feels when going down into some damp, cold vault or cellar.

'A strong shiver shook me from head to foot. Before even I saw it I *knew* that it was there.

'It leant over the railing of the gallery and looked down at us all just as it had done before. There was no change in the attitude, no alteration in the fixed, malignant glare in those stony, lifeless eyes; no movement in the white and bloodless features. Below, amongst the eight of us gathered there, there arose a panic of terror. Eight strong, healthy, well-educated nineteenth-century Englishmen, and yet I am not ashamed to say that we were paralysed with fear. Then one, more quickly recovering his senses than the rest, caught at his gun, that leant against the wide chimney-corner, and fired.

'The hall was filled with smoke, but as it cleared away every one of us could see the figure of our supernatural visitant slowly backing, as he had done on the previous occasion, into the chamber behind him, with something like a sardonic smile of scornful derision upon his horrible, death-like face.

'The next morning it is a singular and remarkable fact that four out of the eight of us received by the morning post—so they stated—letters of importance which called them up to town by the very first train! One man's mother was ill, another had to consult his lawyer, whilst pressing engagements, to which they could assign no definite name, called away the other two.

'There were left in the house that day but four of us— Wells, Bob Harford, our host, and myself. A sort of dogged determination not to be worsted by a scare of this kind kept us still there. The morning light brought a return of common sense and of natural courage to us. We could manage to laugh over last night's terrors whilst discussing our bacon and kidneys and hot coffee over the late breakfast in the pleasant morning-room, with the sunshine streaming cheerily in through the diamond-paned windows.

'It *must* be a delusion of our brains,' said one.

'Our host's champagne,' suggested another.

'A well-organized hoax,' opined a third.

'I will tell you what we will do,' said our host. 'Now that those other fellows have all gone—and I suppose we don't any of us believe much in those elaborate family reasons which have so unaccountably summoned them away—we four will sit up regularly night after night and watch for this thing, whatever it may be. I do not believe in ghosts. However, this morning I have taken the trouble to go out before breakfast to the Rector of the parish, an old gentleman who is well up in all the traditions of the neighbourhood, and I have learnt from him the whole of the supposed story of our friend of the tawny beard, which, if you like, I will relate to you.'

'Henderson then proceeded to tell us the tradition concerning the Dennis Varley who murdered his sister, the nun—a story which I will not repeat to you, Lester, as I see you know it already.

'The clergyman had furthermore told him that the figure of the murdered nun was also sometimes seen in the same gallery, but that this as a very rare occurrence. When both murderer and his victim are seen together terrible misfortunes are sure to assail the unfortunate living man who sees them; and if the nun's face is revealed death within the year is the doom of the ill-fated person who has seen it.

"'Of course," concluded our host, "I consider all these stories to be absolutely childish. At the same time I cannot help thinking that some human agency—probably a gang of thieves or housebreakers—is at work, and that we shall probably be able to unearth an organized system of villainy by which the rogues, presuming on the credulity of the persons who have inhabited the place, have been able to plant themselves securely among some secret passages and hidden rooms in the house, and have carried on their depredations undiscovered and unsuspected. Now, will all of you help me to unravel this mystery?"

'We all promised readily to do so. It is astonishing how brave we felt at eleven o'clock in the morning; what an amount of pluck and courage each man professed himself to be endued with; how lightly we jested about the 'old boy with the beard,' and what jokes we cracked about the murdered nun!

"'She would show her face oftener if she was good-looking. No fear of her looking at Bob Harford, he was too ugly. It was Jack Darent who was the showman of the party; she'd be sure to make straight for him if she could, he was always run after by the women," and so on, till we were all laughing loudly and heartily over our own witticisms. That was eleven o'clock in the morning.

'At eleven o'clock at night we could have given a very different report of ourselves.

'At eleven o'clock at night each man took up his appointed post in solemn and somewhat depressed silence.

'The plan of our campaign had been carefully organized by our host. Each man was posted separately with about thirty yards between them, so that no optical delusion, such as an effect of firelight upon the oak panelling, nor any reflection from the circular mirror over the chimney-piece, should be able to deceive more than one of us. Our host fixed himself in the very centre of the hall, facing the gallery at the end; Wells took up his position halfway up the short, straight flight of steps; Harford was at the top of the stairs upon the gallery itself; I was opposite to him at the further end. In this manner, whenever the figure—ghost or burglar—should appear, it must necessarily be between two of us, and be seen from both the right and the left side. We were prepared to believe that one amongst us might be deceived by his senses or by his imagination, but it was clear that two persons could not see the same object from a different point of view and be simultaneously deluded by any effect of light or any optical hallucination.

'Each man was provided with a loaded revolver, a brandy and soda and a sufficient stock of pipes or cigars to last him through the night. We took up our position at eleven o'clock exactly, and waited.

'At first we were all four very silent and, as I have said before, slightly depressed; but as the hour wore away and nothing was seen or heard we began to talk to each other. Talking, however, was rather a difficulty. To begin with, we had to shout—at least we in the gallery had to shout to Henderson, down in the hall; and though Harford and Wells could converse quite comfortably, I, not being able to see the latter at all from my end of the gallery; had to pass my remarks to him second-hand through Harford, who amused himself in misstating every intelligent remark that I entrusted him with; added to which natural impediments to the "flow of the soul," the elements thought fit to create such a hullabaloo without that conversation was rendered still further work of difficulty.

'I never remember such a night in all my life. The rain came down in torrents; the wind howled and shrieked wildly amongst the tall chimneys and the bare elm trees without. Every now and then there was a lull, and then, again and again, a long sobbing moan came swirling round and round the house, for all the world like the cry of a human being in agony. It was a night to make one shudder, and thank Heaven for a roof over one's head.

'We all sat on at our separate posts hour after hour, listening to the wind and talking at intervals; but as the time wore on insensibly we became less and less talkative, and a sort of depression crept over us.

'At last we relapsed into a profound silence; then suddenly there came upon us all that chill blast of air, like a breath from a charnel-house, that we had experienced before, and almost simultaneously a hoarse cry broke from Henderson in the body of the hall below, and from Wells halfway up the stairs.

'Harford and I sprang to our feet, and we too saw it.

'The dead man was slowly coming up the stairs. He passed silently up with a sort of still, gliding motion, within a few inches of poor Wells, who shrank back, white with terror, against the wall. Henderson rushed wildly up the staircase in pursuit, whilst Harford and I, up on the gallery, fell instinctively back at his approach.

'He passed between us. We saw the glitter of his sightless eyes—the shrivelled skin upon his withered face—the mouth that tell away like the mouth of a corpse, beneath his tawny beard. We felt the cold death-like blast that came with him, and the sickening horror of his terrible presence. Ah! can I ever forget it?'

With a strong shudder Jack Darent buried his face in his hands, and seemed too much overcome for some minutes to be able to proceed.

'My dear fellow, are you *sure*?' I said in an awestruck whisper. He lifted his head.

'Forgive me, Lester; the whole business has shaken my nerves so thoroughly that I have not yet been able to get over it. But I have not yet told you the worst.'

'Good heavens—is there worse?' I ejaculated.

He nodded.

'No sooner,' he continued, 'had this awful creature passed us that Harford clutched at my arm and pointed to the farther end of the gallery.

'"Look!" he cried hoarsely, the nun!

'There, coming towards us from the opposite direction, was the veiled figure of a nun.

'There were the long, flowing black and white garments— the gleam of the crucifix at her neck—the jangle of her rosary-beads from her waist; but her face was hidden.

'A sort of desperation seized me. With a violent effort over myself, I went towards this fresh apparition.'

'It *must* be a hoax,' I said to myself, and there was a half-formed intention in my mind of wrenching aside the flowing draperies and of seeing for myself who and what it was. I strode towards the figure, I stood within half a yard of it. The nun raised her head slowly—and, Lester—*I saw her face!*'

There was a moment's silence.

'What was it like, Jack?' I asked him presently.

He shook his head.

'That I can never tell to any living creature.'

'Was it so horrible?'

He nodded assent, shuddering.

'And what happened next?'

'I believe I fainted. At all events I remembered nothing

further. They made me go to the vicarage the next day. I was so knocked over by it all—I was quite ill. I could not have stayed in the house. I stopped there all yesterday, and I got up to town this morning. I wish to Heaven I had taken your advice, old man, and had never gone to that horrible house.'

'I wish you had, Jack,' I answered fervently, 'Do you know that I shall die within the year?' he asked me presently.

I tried to pooh-pooh it.

'My dear fellow, don't take the thing so seriously as all that. Whatever may be the meaning of these horrible apparitions, there can be nothing but an old wife's fable in that saying. Why on earth should you die—you of all people, a great strong fellow with a constitution of iron? You don't look much like dying!'

'For all that I shall die. I cannot tell you why I am so certain— but I know that it will be so,' he answered in a low voice. 'And some terrible misfortune will happen to Harford— the other two never saw her—it is he and I who are doomed.'

◆

A year has passed away. Last summer fashionable society rang for a week or more with the tale of poor Bob Harford's misfortune. The girl whom he was engaged to, and to whom he was devotedly attached—young, beautiful and wealthy—ran away on the eve of her wedding-day with a drinking, swindling villain who had been turned out of ever so many clubs and tabooed for ages by every respectable man in town, and who had nothing but a handsome face and a fascinating manner to recommend him, and who by dint of these had succeeded in gaining a complete ascendancy over the fickle heart of poor Bob's lovely fiancée. As to Harford, he sold out and went off to the backwoods of Canada, and has never been heard of since.

And what of Jack Darent? Poor, handsome Jack, with his tall figure and his bright, happy face, and the merry blue eyes that had wiled Bella Lester's heart away! Alas! Far away in Southern Africa, poor Jack Darent lies in an unknown grave—slain by a Zulu assegai on the fatal plain of Isandula! And Bella goes about clad in sable garments, heavy-eyed and stricken with sore grief. A widow in heart, if not in name.

HOICHI THE EARLESS

Lafcadio Hearn

More than seven hundred years ago, at Dan-no-ura, in the Straits of Shimonoséki, was fought the last battle of the long contest between the Heiké, or Taira clan, and the Genji, or Minamoto clan. There the Heiké perished utterly, with their women and children, and their infant emperor likewise— now remembered as Antoku Tenno. And that sea and shore have been haunted for seven hundred yeats... Elsewhere I told you about the strange crabs found there, called Heiké crabs, which have human faces on their backs, and are said to be the spirits of Heiké warriors. But there are many strange things to be seen and heard along that coast. On dark nights thousands of ghostly fires hover about the beach, or flit above the waves—pale lights which the fishermen call *Oni-bi,* or demon-fires; and, whenever the winds are up, a sound of great shouting comes from that sea, like a clamour of battle.

In former years the Heiké were much more restless than they are now. They would rise about ships passing in the night, and try to sink them; and at all times they would watch for swimmers, to pull them down. It was in order to appease those dead that the

Buddhist temple, Amidaji, was built at Akamagaséki. A cemetery was also made close by, near the beach; and within it were set up monuments inscribed with the names of the drowned emperor and of his great vassals; and Buddhist services were regularly performed there, on behalf of the spirits. After the temple had been built, and the tombs erected, the Heiké gave less trouble than before; but they continued to do queer things at intervals—proving that they had not found perfect peace.

Some centuries ago, there lived at Akamagaséki a blind man named Höichi, who was famed for his skill in recitation and in playing upon the *biwa*. From childhood he had been trained to recite and to play; and while yet a lad, he had surpassed his teachers. As a professional *biwa-höshi*/aéshi he became famous chiefly by his recitations of the history of the Heiké and the Genji; and it is said that when he sang the song of the battle of Dan-no-ura 'even the goblins [*kijin*] could not refrain from tears'.

At the outset of his career, Höichi was very poor; but he found a good friend to help him. The priest of the Amidaji was fond of poetry and music; and he often invited Höichi to the temple, to play and recite. Afterwards, being much impressed by the wonderful skill of the lad, the priest proposed that Höichi should make the temple his home; and this offer was gratefully accepted. Höichi was given a room in the temple-building; and, in return for food and lodging, he was required only to gratify the priest with a musical performance on certain evenings, when otherwise disengaged.

One summer night the priest was called away to perform a Buddhist service at the house of a dead parishioner; and he went there with his acolyte, leaving Höichi alone in the temple. It was a hot night; and the blind man sought to cool himself on the verandah before his sleeping-room. The verandah overlooked a small garden in the rear of the Amidaji. There Hōichi waited for the priest's return, and tried to relieve his solitude by practising upon his *biwa*. Midnight passed; and the priest did not appear. But the atmosphere was still too warm for comfort within doors; and Hōichi remained outside. At last he heard steps approaching from the back gate. Somebody crossed the garden, advanced to the verandah, and halted directly in front of him—but it was not the priest. A deep voice called the blind man's name—abruptly and unceremoniously, in the manner of a Samurai summoning an inferior:—

'Hōichi!'

Hōichi was too startled for the moment to respond; and the voice called again, in a tone of harsh command—

'Hōichi!'

'*Hai!*' answered the blind man, frightened by the menace in the voice—'I am blind!—I cannot know who calls!'

'There is nothing to fear,' the stranger exclaimed, speaking more gently. 'I am stopping near this temple, and have been sent to you with a message. My present lord, a person of exceedingly high rank, is now staying in Akamagaséki, with many noble attendants. He wished to view the scene of the battle of Dan-no-ura; and today he visited that place. Having heard of your skill in reciting the story of the battle, he now desires to hear your performance: so you will take your *biwa* and come with me at once to the house where the august assembly is waiting.'

In those times, the order of a Samurai was not to be lightly disobeyed. Hōichi donned his sandals, took his *biwa*, and went away with the stranger, who guided him deftly but obliged him to walk very fast. The hand that guided was iron; and the clank of the warrior's stride proved him fully armed—probably some palace-guard on duty. Hōichi first alarm was over: he began to imagine himself in good luck; for, remembering the retainer's assurance about a 'person of exceedingly high rank', he thought that the lord who wished to hear the recitation could not be less than a daimyo of the first class. Presently the Samurai halted; and Höichi became aware that they had arrived at a large gateway; and he wondered, for he could not remember any large gate in that part of the town, except the main gate of the Amidaji. 'Kaimon!' the samurai called—and there was a sound of unbarring; and the twain passed on. They traversed a space of garden, and halted again before an entrance; and the retainer cried in a loud voice, 'Within there! I have brought Höichi.' Then came the sounds of feet hurrying, and screens sliding, and rain-doors opening, and voices of women. By the language of the women Höichi knew them to be domestics in some noble household; but he could not imagine to what place he had been conducted. Little time was allowed him for conjecture. After he had been helped to mount several stone steps, upon the last of which he was told to leave his sandals, a woman's hand guided him along interminable reaches of polished planking and round pillared angles, too many to remember, and over amazing widths of matted floor, into the middle of some vast apartment. There he thought that many great people were assembled: the sound of the rustling of silk was like the sound of leaves in a forest. He heard also a great humming of voices—talking in undertones; and the speech was the speech of courts.

Höichi was told to put himself at ease, and he found a kneeling-cushion ready for him. After having taken his place upon it, and tuned his instrument, the voice of a woman—whom he divined to be the *Röjo*, or matron in charge of the female service—addressed him saying—

'It is now required that the history of the Höichi be recited, to the accompaniment of the *biwa.*'

Now the entire recital would have required a time of many nights; therefore Hōichi ventured a question:—

'As the whole of the story is not soon told, what portion is it augustly desired that I now recite?'

The woman's voice made the answer:—

'Recite the story of the battle at Dan-no-ura—for the pity of it is the most deep.'

Then Hōichi lifted his voice, and chanted the chant of the fight on the bitter sea, wonderfully making his *biwa* sound like the straining of oars and the rushing of ships, the whirr and the hissing of arrows, the shouting and trampling of men, the crashing of steel upon helmets, the plunging of the slain in the flood. And to the left and right of him, in the pauses of his playing, he could hear voices murmuring praise: 'How marvellous an artist!'—'Never in our own province was playing heard like this!'—'Not in all the empire is there another singer like Hōichi!' Then fresh courage came to him, and he played and sang yet better than before; and a hush of wonder deepened about him. But when at last he came to tell the fate of the fair and the helpless, the piteous perishing of the women and children, and the death-leap of Nii-no-Ania, with the imperial infant in her arms, all the listeners uttered together one long, long shuddering cry of anguish; and thereafter they wept and wailed so loudly and so wildly that the blind man was frightened by the violence of the grief that he had made. For much time the sobbing and the wailing continued. But gradually the sounds of lamentation died away; and again, in the great stillness that followed, Hōichi heard the voice of the woman whom he supposed to be the *Rōjo*.

She said:—

'Although we had been assured that you were a very skilful player upon the *biwa*, and without an equal in recitative, we did not know that anyone could be so skilful as you have proved yourself tonight. Our lord has been pleased to say that he intends to bestow upon you a fitting reward. But he desires that you shall perform before him once every night for the next six nights—after which time he will probably make his august return journey. Tomorrow night, therefore, you are to come here at the same hour. The retainer who tonight conducted you will be sent for you. There is another matter about which I have been ordered to inform you. It is required that you shall speak to no one of your visits here, during the time of our lords' august sojourn at Akamagaséki. As he is travelling incognito, he commands that no mention of these things be made. You are now free to go back to your temple.'

After Höichi had duly expressed his thanks, a woman's hand conducted him to the entrance of the house, where the same retainer, who had before guided him, was waiting to take him home. The retainer led him to the verandah at the rear of the temple, and there bade him farewell.

It was almost dawn when Höichi returned; but his absence from the temple had not been observed, as the priest, coming back at a very late hour, had supposed him asleep. During the day Höichi was able to take some rest; and he said nothing about his strange adventure. In the middle of the following night, the samurai again came for him, and led him to the august assembly, where he gave another recitation with the same success that had attended his previous performance. But during this second visit his absence from the temple was accidentally discovered; and after his return in the morning, he was summoned to the presence of the priest, who said to him in a tone of kindly reproach:—

'We have been very anxious about you, friend Hōichi. To go out, blind and alone, at so late an hour, is dangerous. Why did you go without telling us? I could have ordered a servant to accompany you. And where have you been?'

Hōichi answered, evasively—

'Pardon me, kind friend! I had to attend to some private business; and I could not arrange the matter at any other hour.'

The priest was surprised, rather than pained, by Hōichi's reticence; he felt it to be unnatural, and suspected something wrong. He feared that the blind lad had been bewitched or deluded by some evil spirits. He did not ask any more questions; but he privately instructed the men-servants of the temple to keep watch upon Hōichi's movements, and to follow him in case he should again leave the temple after dark.

On the very next night, Hōichi was seen to leave the temple; and the servants immediately lighted their lanterns, and followed him. But it was a rainy night, and very dark; and before the temple-folks could get to the roadway Hōichi had disappeared. Evidently he had walked very fast—a strange thing, considering his blindness; for the road was in a bad condition. The men hurried through the streets, making inquiries at every house which Hōichi was accustomed to visit; but nobody could give them any news of him. At last, as they were returning to the temple by way of the shore, they were startled by the sound of a *biwa*, furiously played, in the cemetery of the Amidaji. Except for some ghostly fires—such as usually flitted there on dark nights—all was blackness in that direction. But the men at once hastened to the cemetery; and there, by the help of their lanterns, they discovered Hōichi—sitting alone in the rain before the memorial tomb of Antuko Tenno, making his *biwa* resound, and loudly chanting the chant of the battle of Dan-no-ura. And behind him, and about him, and everywhere above the tombs, the fires of the dead were burning, like candles. Never before had so great a host of *Oni-bi* appeared in the sight of mortal man...

'Höichi San!—Höichi San!' the servants cried, 'You are bewitched!... Höichi San!'

But the blind man did not seem to hear. Strenuously he made his *biwa* rattle and ring and clang; more wildly he chanted the chant of the battle of Dan-no-ura. They caught hold of him and shouted into his ear—

'Höichi San!—Höichi San!—come home with us at once!' Reprovingly he spoke to them:—

'To interrupt me in such a manner, before this august assembly, will not be tolerated.'

Whereat, in spite of the weirdness of the thing, the servants could not help laughing. Sure that he had been bewitched, they now seized him, and pulled him up on his feet, and by force hurried him back to the temple, where he was immediately relieved of his wet clothes, by order of the priest, and reclad, and made to eat and drink. Then the priest insisted upon a full explanation of his friend's astonishing behaviour.

Höichi long hesitated to speak. But at last, finding that his conduct had really alarmed and angered the good priest, he decided to abandon his reserve; and he related everything that had happened from the time of the first visit of the samurai.

The priest said:—

'Höichi, my poor friend, you are now in great danger! How unfortunate that you did not tell me all this before! Your wonderful skill in music has indeed brought you strange trouble. By this time you must be aware that you have not been visiting any house whatever, but have been passing your nights in the cemetery, among the tombs of the Heiké; and it was before the memorial-tomb of Antoku Tenno that our people tonight found you, sitting in the rain. All that you have been imagining was illusion—except the calling of the dead. By once obeying them, you have put yourself in their power. If you obey them again, after what has already occurred, they will tear you to pieces. But they would have destroyed you, sooner or later, in any event. Now I shall not be able to remain with you tonight: I am called away to perform another service. But, before I go, it will be necessary to protect your body by writing holy texts upon it.'

Before sundown the priest and his acolyte stripped Höichi: then, with their writing-brushes, they traced upon his breast and back, head and face and neck, limbs and hands and feet even upon the soles of his feet, and upon all parts of his body—the text of the holy sûtra called *Hannya-Shin-Kyö*. When this had been done, the priest instructed Höichi, saying:—

'Tonight, as soon as I go away, you must seat yourself on the verandah, and wait. You will be called. But whatever may happen, do not answer, and do not move. Say nothing, and sit still—as if meditating. If you stir, or make any noise, you will be torn asunder. Do not get frightened; and do not think of calling for help—because no help could save you. If you do exactly as I tell you, the danger will pass, and you will have nothing more to fear.'

After dark, the priest and the acolyte went away; and Höichi sat himself on the verandah, according to the instructions given him. He laid his *biwa* on the planking beside him, and, assuming the attitude of meditation, remained quite still—taking care not to cough, or to breathe audibly. For hours he stayed thus.

Then, from the roadway, he heard the steps coming. They

passed the gate, crossed the garden, approached the verandah, stopped directly in front of him.

'Höichi!' the deep voice called. But the blind man held his breath, and sat motionless.

'Höichi!' grimly called the voice a second time. Then a third time, savagely:—

'Höichi!'

Höichi remained as still as a stone, and the voice grumbled— 'No answer!—that won't do... Must see where the fellow is.'

There was a noise of heavy feet mounting upon the verandah. The feet approached deliberately, and halted beside him. Then, for long minutes, during which Höichi felt his whole body shake to the beating of his heart, there was dead silence.

At last the gruff voice muttered close to him:—

'Here is the *biwa*; but of its player I see—only two ears!... So that explains why he did not answer: he had no mouth to answer with—there is nothing left of him but his ears... Now to my lord those ears I will take in proof that the august commands have been obeyed, so far as was possible.'

At that instant Höichi felt his ears gripped by fingers of iron, and torn off! Great as the pain was, he gave no cry. The heavy footfalls receded along the verandah, descended into the garden, passed out to the roadway and ceased. From either side of his head, the blind man felt a thick, warm liquid trickling; but he dared not lift his hands.

Before sunrise the priest came back. He hastened at once to the verandah in the rear, stepped and slipped upon something clammy, and uttered a cry of horror, for he saw, by the light of his lantern, that the clamminess was blood. But he perceived Höichi sitting there, in the attitude of meditation—With the blood still oozing from his wounds.

'My poor Hōichi!' cried the startled priest, 'what is this? You have been hurt?'

At the sound of his friend's voice, the blind man felt safe. He burst out sobbing, and tearfully told his adventure of the night.

'Poor, poor Hōichi!' the priest exclaimed, 'all my fault! My very grievous fault! Everywhere upon your body the holy texts had been written—except upon your ears! I trusted my acolyte to do that part of the work; and it was very, very wrong of me not to have made sure that he had done it!... Well, the matter cannot now be helped; we can only try to heal your wounds as soon as possible. Cheer up, friend! The danger is now well over. You will never again be troubled by those visitors.'

With the aid of a good doctor, Hōichi soon recovered from his injuries. The story of his strange adventure spread far and wide, and soon made him famous. Many noble persons went to Akamagaséki to hear him recite; and large presents of money were given to him, so that he became a wealthy man. But from the time of his adventure, he was known only by the appellation of *Mimi-nashi-Hōichi:* 'Hōichi-the-Earless'.

THE EMPTY HOUSE

Algernon Blackwood

Certain houses, like certain persons, manage somehow to proclaim at once their character for evil. In the case of the latter, no particular feature need betray them; they may boast an open countenance and an ingenuous smile; and yet a little of their company leaves the unalterable conviction that there is something radically amiss with their being: that they are evil. Willy nilly, they seem to communicate an atmosphere of secret and wicked thoughts which makes those in their immediate neighbourhood shrink from them as from a thing diseased.

And, perhaps, with houses the same principle is operative, and it is the aroma of evil deeds committed under a particular roof, long after the actual doers have passed away that makes the gooseflesh come and the hair rise. Something of the original passion of the evil-doer, and of the horror felt by his victim, enters the heart of the innocent watcher, and he becomes suddenly conscious of tingling nerves, creeping skin, and a chilling of the blood. He is terror-stricken without apparent cause.

There was manifestly nothing in the external appearance

of this particular house to bear out the tales of the horror that was said to reign within. It was neither lonely nor unkempt. It stood, crowded into a corner of the square, and looked exactly like the houses on either side of it. It had the same number of windows as its neighbours; the same balcony overlooking the gardens; the same white steps leading up to the heavy black front door; and, in the rear, there was the same narrow strip of green, with neat box borders, running up to the wall that divided it from the backs of the adjoining houses. Apparently too, the number of chimney pots on the roof was the same; the breadth and angle of the eaves; and even the height of the dirty area railings.

And yet this house in the square, that seemed precisely similar to its fifty ugly neighbours, was as a matter of fact entirely different—horribly different.

Wherein lay this marked, invisible difference is impossible to say. It cannot be ascribed wholly to the imagination, because persons who had spent some time in the house, knowing nothing of the facts, had declared positively that certain rooms were so disagreeable they would rather die than enter them again, and that the atmosphere of the whole house produced in them symptoms of a genuine terror; while the series of innocent tenants who had tried to live in it and been forced to decamp at the shortest possible notice, was indeed little less than a scandal in the town.

When Shorthouse arrived to pay a 'week-end' visit to his Aunt Julia in her little house on the sea-front at the other end of the town, he found her charged to the brim with mystery and excitement. He had only received her telegram that morning, and he had come anticipating boredom; but the moment he touched her hand and kissed her apple-skin wrinkled cheek, he caught the first waves of her electrical condition. The impression deepened when he learned that there were to be no other visitors, and that he had been telegraphed for with a very special object.

Something was in the wind, and the 'something' would doubtless bear fruit; for this elderly spinster aunt, with a mania for psychical research, had brains as well as willpower, and by hook or by crook she usually managed to accomplish her ends. The revelation was made soon after tea, when she sidled close up to him as they paced slowly along the sea-front in the dusk.

'I've got the keys,' she announced in a delighted, yet half awesome voice. 'Got them till Monday!'

'The keys of the bathing-machine, or—?' he asked innocently, looking from the sea to the town. Nothing brought her so quickly to the point as feigning stupidity.

'Neither,' she whispered. 'I've got the keys of the haunted house in the square—and I'm going there tonight.'

Shorthouse was conscious of the slightest possible tremor down his hack. He dropped his teasing tone. Something in her voice and manner thrilled him. She was in earnest.

'But you can't go alone—' he began.

'That's why I wired for you,' she said with decision.

He turned to look at her. The ugly, lined, enigmatical face was alive with excitement. There was the glow of genuine enthusiasm round it like halo. The eyes shone. He caught another wave of her excitement, and a second tremor, more marked than the first, accompanied it.

'Thanks, Aunt Julia,' he said politely; 'thanks awfully.'

'I should not dare to go quite alone,' she went on, raising her voice; 'But with you I should enjoy it immensely. You're afraid of nothing, I know.'

'Thanks *so* much,' he said again. 'Er—is anything likely to happen?'

'A great deal *has* happened,' she whispered, 'though it's been most cleverly hushed up. Three tenants have come and gone in the last few months, and the house is said to be empty for good now.'

In spite of himself Shorthouse became interested. His aunt was so very much in earnest.

'The house is very old indeed,' she went on, 'and the story—an unpleasant one—dates a long way back. It has to do with a murder committed by a jealous stableman who had some affair with a servant in the house. One night he managed to secrete himself in the cellar, and when everyone was asleep, he crept upstairs to the servants' quarters, chased the girl down to the next landing, and before anyone could come to the rescue threw her bodily over the banisters into the hall below.'

'And the stableman—?'

'Was caught, I believe, and hanged for murder; but it all happened a century ago, and I've not been able to get more details of the story.'

Shorthouse now felt his interest thoroughly aroused but, though he was not particularly nervous for himself, he hesitated a little on his aunt's account.

'On one condition,' he said at length.

'Nothing will prevent my going,' she said firmly; 'but I may as well hear your condition.'

'That you guarantee your power of self-control if anything really horrible happens. I mean—that you are sure you won't get too frightened.'

'Jim,' she said scornfully, 'I'm not young, I know, nor are my nerves; but *with you* I should be afraid of nothing in the world!'

This, of course, settled it, for Shorthouse had no pretensions to being other than a very ordinary young man, and an appeal to his vanity was irresistible. He agreed to go.

Instinctively, by a sort of subconscious preparation, he kept himself and his forces well in hand the whole evening, compelling an accumulative reserve of control by that nameless inward process of gradually putting all the emotions away and turning the key upon them—a process difficult to describe, but wonderfully effective, as all men who have lived through severe trials of the inner man well understand. Later, it stood him in good stead.

But it was not until half-past ten, when they stood in the hall, well in the glare of friendly lamps and still surrounded by comforting human influences, that he had to make the first call upon this store of collected strength. For, once the door was closed, and he saw the deserted silent street stretching away white in the moonlight before them, it came to him clearly that the real test that night would he in dealing with *two fears* instead of one. He would have to carry his aunt's fear as well as his own. And, as he glanced down at her sphinx-like countenance and realized that it might assume no pleasant aspect in a rush of real terror, he felt satisfied with only one thing in the whole adventure—that he had confidence in his own will and power to stand against any shock that might come.

Slowly they walked along the empty streets of the town; a bright autumn moon silvered the roofs, casting deep shadows; there was no breath of wind; and the trees in the formal gardens by the sea-front watched them silently as they passed along. To his aunt's occasional remarks Shorthouse made no reply, realizing that she was simply surrounding herself with mental buffers—saying ordinary things to prevent herself thinking of extraordinary things. Few windows showed lights, and from scarcely a single chimney came smoke or sparks. Shorthouse had already begun to notice everything, even the smallest details. Presently they stopped at the street corner and looked up at the name on the side of the house full in the moonlight, and with one accord, but without remark, turned into the square and crossed over to the side of it that lay in shadow.

'The number of the house is thirteen,' whispered a voice at his side; and neither of them made the obvious reference, but passed across the broad sheet of moonlight and began to march up the pavement in silence.

It was about halfway up the square that Shorthouse felt an arm slipped quietly but significantly into his own, and knew then that their adventure had begun in earnest, and that his companion was already yielding imperceptibly to the influences against them. She needed support.

A few minutes later they stopped before a tall, narrow house that rose before them into the night, ugly in shape and painted a dingy white, shutterless windows, without blinds, stared down upon them, shining here and there in the moonlight. There were weather streaks in the wall and cracks in the paint, and the balcony bulged out from the first floor a little unnaturally. But, beyond this generally forlorn appearance of an unoccupied house, there was nothing at first sight to single out this particular mansion for the evil character it had most certainly acquired.

Taking a look over their shoulders to make sure they had not been followed, they went boldly up the steps and stood against the huge black door that fronted them forbiddingly. But the first wave of nervousness was now upon them, and Shorthouse fumbled a long time with the key before he could fit it into the lock at all. For a moment, if truth were told, they both hoped it would not open, for they were a prey to various unpleasant emotions as they stood there on the threshold of their ghostly adventure. Shorthouse, shuttling with the key and hampered by the steady weight on his arm, certainly felt the solemnity of the moment. It was as if the whole world—for all experience seemed at that instant concentrated in his own consciousness—were listening to the grating noise of that key. A stray puff of wind wandering down the empty street woke a momentary rustling in the trees behind them, but otherwise this rattling of the key was the only sound audible; and at last it turned in the lock and the heavy door swung open and revealed a yawning gulf of darkness beyond.

With a last glance at the moonlit square, they passed quickly in, and the door slammed behind them with a roar that echoed prodigiously through empty halls and passages. But, instantly, with the echoes, another sound made itself heard, and Aunt Julia leaned suddenly so heavily upon him that he had to take a step backwards to save himself from falling.

A man had coughed close beside them—so close that it seemed they must have been actually by his side in the darkness.

With the possibility of practical jokes in his mind, Shorthouse at once swung his heavy stick in the direction of the sound; but it met nothing more solid than air. He heard his aunt give a little gasp beside him.

'There's someone here,' she whispered, 'I heard him.'

'Be quiet!' he said sternly. 'It was nothing but the noise of the front door.'

'Oh! Get a light—quick!' she added, as her nephew, fumbling; with a box of matches, opened it upside down and let them all fall with a rattle on to the stone floor.

The sound, however, was not repeated; and there was no

evidence of retreating footsteps. In another minute they had a candle burning; using an empty end of a cigar case as a holder; and when the first flare had died down he held the impromptu lamp aloft and surveyed the scene. And it was dreary enough in all conscience, for there is nothing more desolate in all the abodes of men than an unfurnished house dimly lit, silent, and forsaken, and yet tenanted by rumour with the memories of evil and violent histories.

They were standing in a wide hall-way; on their left was the open door of a spacious dining-room, and in front the hall ran, ever narrowing, into a long, dark passage that led apparently to the top of the kitchen stairs. The broad uncarpeted staircase rose in a sweep before them, everywhere draped in shadows, except for a single spot about halfway up where the moonlight came in through the window and fell on a bright patch on the boards. This shaft of light shed a faint radiance above and below it, lending to the objects within its reach a misty outline that was infinitely more suggestive and ghostly than complete darkness. Filtered moonlight always seems to paint faces on the surrounding gloom, and as Shorthouse peered up into the well of darkness and thought of the countless empty rooms and passages in the upper part of the old house, he caught himself longing again for the safety of the moonlit square, or the cosy; bright drawing-room they had left an hour before. Then realizing that these thoughts were dangerous, he thrust them away again and summoned all his energy for concentration on the present.

'Aunt Julia,' he said aloud, severely, 'we must now go through the house from top to bottom and make a thorough search.'

The echoes of his voice died away slowly all over the building, and in the intense silence that followed he turned to look at her. In the candlelight he saw that her face was already ghastly pale; but she dropped his arm for a moment and said in a whisper, stepping close in front of him—

'I agree. We must be sure there's no one hiding. That's the first thing.'

She spoke with evident effort, and he looked at her with admiration.

'You feel quite sure of yourself? It's not too late—'

'I think so,' she whispered, her eyes shifting nervously toward the shadows behind. 'Quite sure, only one thing—'

'What's that.'

'You must never leave me alone for an instant.'

'As long as you understand that any sound or appearance must he investigated at once, for to hesitate means to admit fear. That is fatal.'

'Agreed,' she said, little shakily, after a moment's hesitation. 'I'll try—'

Arm in arm, Shorthouse holding the dripping candle and the stick, while his aunt carried the cloak over her shoulders, figures of utter comedy to all but themselves, they began a systematic search.

Stealthily, walking, on tip-toe and shading the candle lest it should betray their presence through the shutterless windows, they went first into the big dining-room. There was not a stick of furniture to be seen. Bare walls, ugly mantel-pieces and empty grates stared at them. Everything, they felt resented their intrusion, watching them, as it were, with veiled eyes; whispers followed them; shadows flirted noiselessly to right and left; something seemed ever at their hack, watching, waiting an opportunity to do them injury. There was the inevitable sense that operations which went on when the room was empty had been temporarily suspended till they were well out of the way again. The whole dark interior of the old building seemed to become a malignant presence that rose up, warning them to desist and mind their own business; every moment the strain on the nerves increased.

Out of the gloomy dining-room they passed through large folding doors into a sort of library or smoking-room, wrapt equally in silence, darkness, and dust; and from this they regained the hall near the top of the back stairs.

Here a pitch black tunnel opened before them into the lower regions, and—it must be confessed—they hesitated. But only for a minute. With the worst of the night still to come it was essential to turn from nothing. Aunt Julia stumbled at the top step of the dark descent, ill lit by the flickering candle, and even Shorthouse felt at least half the decision go out of his legs.

'Come on!' he said peremptorily, and his voice ran on and lost itself in the dark, empty spaces below.

'I'm coming,' she faltered, catching his arm with unnecessary violence.

They went a little unsteadily down the stone steps, a cold, damp air meeting them in the face, close and malodorous. The kitchen, into which the stairs led along a narrow passage, was large, with a lofty ceiling. Several doors opened out of it—some into cupboards with empty jars still standing on the shelves, and others into horrible little ghostly back offices, each colder and less inviting than the last. Black beetles scurried over the floor, and once, when they knocked against a deal table standing in a corner, something about the size of a cat jumped down with a rush and fled, scampering across the stone floor into the darkness. Everywhere there was a sense of recent occupation, an impression of sadness and gloom.

Leaving the main kitchen, they next went towards the

scullery. The door was standing ajar, and as they pushed it open to its full extent Aunt Julia uttered a piercing scream, which she instantly tried to stifle by placing her hand over her mouth. For a second Shorthouse stood stock-still, catching his breath. He felt as if his spine had suddenly become hollow and someone had filled it with particles of ice.

Facing them, directly in their way between the doorposts, stood the figure of a woman. She had dishevelled hair and wildly staring eyes, and her face was terrified and white as death.

She stood there motionless for the space of a single second. Then the candle flickered and she was gone—gone utterly—and the door framed nothing but empty darkness.

'Only the beastly jumping candlelight,' he said quickly, in a voice that sounded like someone else's and was only half under control. 'Come on, aunt. There's nothing there.'

He dragged her forward. With a clattering of feet and a great appearance of boldness they went on, but over his body the skin moved as if crawling ants covered it, and he knew by the weight on his arm that he was supplying the force of locomotion for two. The scullery was cold, bare, and empty; more like a large prison cell than anything else. They went round it, tried the door into the yard, and the windows, but found them all fastened securely. His aunt moved beside him like a person in a dream. Her eyes were tightly shut, and she seemed merely to follow the pressure of his arm. Her courage filled him with amazement. At the same time he noticed that a certain odd change had come over her face a change which somehow evaded his power of analysis.

'There's nothing here, aunty,' he repeated aloud quickly. 'Let's go upstairs and see the rest of the house. Then we'll choose a room to wait up in.'

She followed him obediently, keeping close to his side, and they locked the kitchen door behind them. It was a relief to get up again. In the hall there was more light than before, for the moon had travelled a little further down the stairs. Cautiously they began to go up into the dark vault of the upper house, the boards creaking under their weight.

On the first floor they found the large double drawing-rooms, a search of which revealed nothing. Here also was no sign of furniture or recent occupancy; nothing but dust and neglect and shadows. They opened the big folding doors between front and back drawing-rooms and then came out again to the landing and went on upstairs.

They had not gone up more than a dozen steps when they both simultaneously stopped to listen, looking into each other's eyes with a new apprehension across the flickering candle flame. From the room they had left hardly ten seconds before came the sound of doors quietly closing. It was beyond all question; they heard the booming noise that accompanies the shutting of heavy doors, followed by the sharp catching of the latch.

'We must go back and see,' said Shorthouse briefly, in a low tone, and turning to go downstairs again.

Somehow she managed to drag after him, her feet catching in her dress, her face livid.

When they entered the front drawing-room it was plain that the folding doors had been closed—half a minute before. Without hesitation Shorthouse opened them. He almost expected to see someone facing him in the back room; but only darkness and cold air met him. They went through both rooms, finding nothing unusual. They tried in every way to make the doors close of themselves, but there was not wind enough even to set the candle flame flickering. The doors would not move without strong pressure. All was silent as the grave. Undeniably the rooms were utterly empty, and the house utterly still.

'It's beginning,' whispered a voice at his elbow which he hardly recognized as his aunt's.

He nodded acquiescence, taking out his watch to note the time. It was fifteen minutes before midnight; he made the entry of exactly what had occurred in his notebook, setting the candle in its case upon the floor in order to do so. It took a moment or two to balance it safely against the wall.

Aunt Julia always declared than at this moment she was not actually watching him, but had turned her head towards the inner room, where she fancied she heard something moving; but, at any rate, both positively agreed that there came a sound of rushing feet, heavy and very swift—and the next instant the candle was out!

But to Shorthouse himself had come more than this, and he has always thanked his fortunate stars that it came to him alone and not in his aunt too. For, as he rose from the stooping position of balancing the candle, and before it was actually extinguished, a face thrust itself forward so close to his own that he could almost have touched it with his lips. It was a face working with passion; a man's face, dark, with thick features, and angry, savage eyes. It belonged to a common man, and it was evil in its ordinary normal expression, no doubt, but as he saw it, alive with intense, aggressive emotion it was a malignant and terrible human countenance.

There was no movement of the air; nothing but the sound of rushing feet—stockinged or muffed feet; the apparition of the face; and the almost simultaneous extinguishing of the candle.

In spite of himself, Shorthouse uttered a little cry, nearly losing his balance as his aunt clung to him with her whole weight in one moment of real, uncontrollable terror. She made no sound, but simply seized him bodily. Fortunately, however, she had seen nothing, but had only heard the rushing feet, for her control returned almost at once, and he was able to disentanble himself and strike a match.

The shadows ran away on all sides before the glare, and his aunt stooped down and groped for the cigar case with the precious candle. Then they discovered that the candle had not been *blown* out at all; it had been *crushed* out. The wick was pressed down into the wax, which was flattened as if by some smooth, heavy instrument.

How his companion so quickly overcame her terror, Shorthouse never properly understood; but his admiration for her self-control increased tenfold, and at the same time served to feed his own dying flame—for which he was undeniably grateful. Equally inexplicable to him was the evidence of physical force they had just witnessed. He at once suppressed the memory of stories he had heard of "physical mediums" and their dangerous phenomena; for if these were true, and either his aunt or himself was unwittingly a physical medium, it meant that they were simply aiding to focus the forces of a haunted house already charged to the brim. It was like walking with unprotected lamps among uncovered stores of gunpowder.

So, with as little reflection as possible, he simply relit the candle and went up to the next floor. The arm in his trembled, it is true, and his own tread was often uncertain, but they went on with thoroughness, and after a search revealing nothing they climbed the last flight of stairs to the top floor of all.

Here they found a perfect nest of small servants' rooms, with broken pieces of furniture, dirty cane-bottomed chairs, chests of drawers, cracked mirrors, and decrepit bedsteads. The rooms had low sloping ceilings already hung here and there with cobwebs, small windows, and badly plastered walls—a depressing and dismal region which they were glad to leave behind.

It was on the stroke of midnight when they entered a small room on the third floor, close to the top of the stairs, and arranged to make themselves comfortable for the remainder of their adventure. It was absolutely bare, and was said to be the room—then used as a clothes closet—into which the infuriated groom had chased his victim and finally caught her. Outside, across the narrow landing, began the stairs leading up to the floor above, and the servants' quarters where they had just searched.

In spite of the chilliness of the night there was something in the air of this room that cried for an open window. But there was more than this. Shorthouse could only describe it by saying that he felt less master of himself here than in any other part of the house. There was something that acted directly on the nerves, tiring the resolution, enfeebling the will. He was conscious of this result before he had been in the room five minutes, and it was in the short time they stayed there that he suffered the wholesale depletion of his vital forces, which was, for himself, the chief horror of the whole experience.

They put the candle on the floor of the cupboard, leaving the door a few inches ajar, so that there was no glare to confuse the eyes, and no shadow to shift about on walls and ceiling. Then they spread the cloak on the floor and sat down to wait, with their backs against the wall.

Shorthouse was within two feet of the door on to the landing; his position commanded a good view of the main staircase leading down into the darkness, and also of the beginning of the servants' stairs going to the floor above; the heavy stick lay beside him within easy reach.

The moon was now high above the house. Through the open window they could see the comforting stars like friendly eyes watching in the sky. One by one the clocks of the town struck midnight, and when the sounds died away the deep silence of a windless night fell again over everything. Only the boom of the sea, far away and lugubrious, filled the air with hollow murmurs.

Inside the house the silence became awful; awful, he thought, because any minute now it might be broken by sounds portending terror. The strain of waiting told more and more severely on the nerves; they talked in whispers when they talked at all, for their voices aloud sounded queer and unnatural. A chilliness, not altogether due to the night air, invaded the room, and made them cold. The influences against them whatever these might be, were slowly robbing them of self-confidence, and the power of decisive action; their forces were on the wane, and the possibility of real fear took on a new and terrible meaning. He began to tremble for the elderly woman by his side, whose pluck could hardly save her beyond a certain extent.

He heard the blood singing in his veins. It sometimes seemed so loud that he fancied it prevented his hearing properly certain other sounds that were beginning very faintly to make themselves audible in the depths of the house. Every time he fastened his attention on these sounds, they instantly ceased. They certainly came no nearer. Yet he could not rid himself of the idea that movement was going on somewhere in the lower regions of the house. The drawing-room floor, where the door had been so strangely closed, seemed too near; the sounds were further off than that. He thought of the great kitchen, with the scurrying black-beetles, and of the dismal little scullery;

but, somehow or other, they did not seem to come from there either. Surely they were not *outside* the house!

Then, suddenly, the truth flashed into his mind, and for the space of a minute he felt as if his blood had stopped flowing and turned to ice.

The sounds were not downstairs at all; they were *upstairs*—upstairs, somewhere among those horrid gloomy little servants' rooms with their bits of broken furniture, low ceilings, and cramped windows—upstairs where the victim had first been disturbed and stalked to her death.

And the moment he discovered where the sounds were, he began to heat them more clearly. It was the sound of feet, moving stealthily along the pass overhead, in and out among the rooms, and past the furniture.

He turned quickly to steal a glance at the motionless figure seated beside him, to note whether she had shared his discovery. The faint candlelight coming through the crack in the cupboard door, threw her strongly-marked face into vivid relief against the white of the wall. But it was something else that made him catch his breath and stare again. An extraordinary something had come into her face and seemed to spread over her features like a mask; it smoothed out the deep lines and drew the skin everywhere a little tighter so that the wrinkles disappeared; it brought into the face—with the sole exception of the old eyes—an appearance of youth and almost of childhood.

He stated in speechless amazement—amazement that was dangerously near to horror. It was his aunt's lace indeed, but it was her face of forty years ago, the vacant innocent face of a girl. He had heard stories of that strange effect of terror which could wipe a human countenance clean of other emotions, obliterating all previous expression; but he had never realized that it could he literally true, or could mean anything so simply horrible as what he now saw. For the dreadful signature of overmastering fear was written plainly in that utter vacancy of the girlish face beside him; and when, feeling, his intense gaze, she turned to look at him, he instinctively closed his eyes tightly to shut out the sight.

Yet, when he turned a minute later, his feelings well in hand, he saw to his intense relief another expression; his aunt was smiling, and though the face was deathly white, the awful veil had lifted and the normal look was returning.

'Anything wrong?' was all he could think of to say at the moment. And the answer was eloquent, coming from such a woman.

'I feel cold—and a little frightened,' she whispered.

He offered to close the window, but she seized hold of him and begged him not to leave her side even for an instant.

'It's upstairs, I know,' she whispered, with an odd half laugh; 'but I can't possibly go up.'

But Shorthouse thought otherwise, knowing that in action lay their best hope of self-control.

He took the brandy flash and poured out a glass of neat spirit, stiff enough to help anybody over anything. She swallowed it with a little shiver. His only idea now was to get out of the house before her collapse became inevitable; but this could not safely be done by turning tail and running from the enemy. Inaction was no longer possible; every minute he was growing less master of himself, and desperate, aggressive measures were imperative without further delay. Moreover, the action must be taken *towards* the enemy, not away from it; the climax, if necessary and unavoidable, would have to be faced boldly. He could do it now; but in ten minutes he might not have the force left to act for himself, much less for both!

Upstairs, the sounds were meanwhile becoming louder and closer, accompanied by occasional creaking of the boards. Someone was moving stealthily about, stumbling now and then awkwardly against the furniture.

Waiting a few moments to allow the tremendous dose of spirits to produce its effect and knowing this would last but a short time under the circumstances, Shorthouse then quietly got on his feet, saying in a determined voice—

'Now, Aunt Julia, we'll go upstairs and find out what all this noise is about. You must come too. It's what we agreed.'

He picked up his stick and went to the cupboard for the candle. A limp form rose shakily beside him breathing hard, and he heard a voice say very faintly something about being 'ready to come'. The woman's courage amazed him; it was so much greater than his own; and, as they advanced, holding aloft the dripping candle, some subtle force exhaled from this trembling, white-laced old woman at his side that was the true source of his inspiration. It held something really great that shamed him and gave him the support without which he would have proved far less equal to the occasion.

They crossed the dark landing, avoiding with their eyes the deep black space over the banisters. Then they began to mount the narrow staircase to meet the sounds which, minute by minute, grew louder and nearer. About halfway up the stairs Aunt Julia stumbled and Shorthouse turned to catch her by the arm, and just at that moment there came terrific crash in the servants' corridor overhead. It was instantly followed by a shrill, agonized scream that was a cry of terror and a cry for help melted into one.

Before they could move aside, or go down a single step,

someone came rushing along the passage overhead, blundering horribly, racing madly, at full speed, three steps at a time, down the very staircase where they stood. The steps were light and uncertain; but close behind them sounded the heavier tread of another person, and the staircase seemed to shake.

Shorthouse and his companion just had time to flatten themselves against the wall when the jumble of flying steps was upon them, and two persons, with the slightest possible interval between them, dashed past at full speed. It was a perfect whirlwind of sound breaking in upon the midnight silence of the empty building.

The two runners, pursuer and pursued, had passed clean through them where they stood, and already with a thud the boards below had received first one, then the other. Yet they had seen absolutely nothing—not a hand, or arm, or face, or even a shred of flying clothing.

There came a second's pause. Then the first one, the lighter of the two, obviously the pursued one, ran with uncertain footsteps into the little room which Shorthouse and his aunt had just left. The heavier one followed. There was a sound of scuffling, gasping, and smothered screaming; and then out on to the landing came the step—of a single person *treading weightily*.

A dead silence followed for the space of half a minute, and then was heard a rushing sound through the air. It was followed by a dull, crashing thud in the depths of the house below—on the stone floor of the hall.

Utter silence reigned after. Nothing moved. The flame of the candle was steady. It had been steady the whole time, and the air had been undisturbed by any movement whatsoever. Palsied with terror, Aunt Julia, without waiting for her companion, began fumbling her way downstairs; she was crying gently to herself, and when Shorthouse put his arm round her and half carried her he felt that she was trembling like a leaf. He went into the little room and picked up the cloak from the floor, and, arm in arm, walking very slowly, without speaking a word or looking once behind them, they marched down; the three flights into the hall.

In the hall they saw nothing, but the whole way down the stairs they were conscious that someone followed them; step by step; when; they went faster IT was left behind, and when they went more slowly IT caught them up. But never once did they look behind to see; and at each turning of the staircase they lowered their eyes for fear of the following horror they might see upon the stairs above.

With trembling hands Shorthouse opened the front door, and they walked out into the moonlight and drew a deep breath of the cool night air blowing in from the sea.

MRS RAEBURN'S WAXWORK

Lady Eleanor Smith

The rain, which had poured with a pitiless ferocity for so long upon the chimneys and roofs of the great manufacturing city, seemed at length to enclose the whole town within towering prison-walls of burnished steel. It was now afternoon; the short winter day was nearly over, and it had rained thus from dawn, would probably continue to rain throughout the night. A dark, wet dusk began to envelop the city like a sable blanket; the street-lamps sprang into life, looming ahead like the ghosts of drowned and weary daffodils, casting watery and trembling reflections upon the shining rivers that were pavements. There were few people walking the mournful streets, and those that were had to struggle and batter their way through sharp gusts of wind, bent double beneath dripping and top-heavy umbrellas.

Such a one was Patrick Lamb, and so great was his hurry that more than once as he stumbled over an unperceived kerb he ran the risk of entangling both himself and his umbrella in the foaming, muddy torrents of the gutters beneath his feet. He had every reason to hurry; he was on his way to apply for a job, and he feared that unless he hastened he would be too late to secure this vacancy which meant so much to him.

Turning at last into a dark and narrow street, he saw opposite to him a ramshackle building of yellow brick, from the roof of which swelled forth a glass dome encrusted with the dirt and soot of ages. A flight of shallow steps led to a swing door. This was his destination.

He flung open the door and was immediately confronted by a turnstile, near which sat a seedy-looking man in an ill-fitting, uniform not unlike that of a fireman.

'Sixpence, please,' said the man, and whistled through his teeth.

Patrick Lamb shook his head.

'No… I'm not a visitor: I have an appointment with Mr Mugivan, the manager.'

'Ah—ha,' said the attendant knowingly, and showed him into a tiny slice of a room filled with papers, files, account-books and dust. Here sat Mr Mugivan, a fat, podgy man with thick legs and a face like a tomato.

'Good afternoon,' said Patrick Lamb hesitatingly, 'I hear that you have a vacancy here for an—an attendant.'

Mr Mugivan stared for a moment at the young man's sallow, rather long face, at his deep-set grey eyes and slender, puny body.

'Who told you so?'

'My landlady, in Bury Street. She knew the last man you had here.'

'And what made you come?'

'Necessity. I'm in need of work. I was stranded here a week ago with a theatrical company.'

There was a silence. Mr Mugivan suddenly laughed, looking at his visitor rather defiantly with little red-rimmed eyes that were not unlike the eyes of a pig.

'Rather a come-down, isn't it, for an actor to find himself minding Mugivan's Waxworks?'

'That doesn't matter—sir. And, if you'll only let me, I'll mind them damn well.'

'It's long hours,' said the proprietor, still speaking contemptuously. 'Nine in the morning till seven at night. An hour for lunch and an hour for tea. Two pounds a week—and the attendant has to wear a uniform. *An actor* wouldn't fancy that, would he?'

'Maybe I'm not an actor,' said Patrick Lamb.

Mr Mugivan spat upon the floor.

'I'll give you a trial, anyhow. What's your name?

Patrick told him.

'Well, Lamb,' and the proprietor creaked himself out of his chair, revealing incidentally that he wore carpet slippers and had bunions, 'come with me and I'll show you Mugivan's Beauties before you go. You can start tomorrow morning.'

Obediently Patrick followed his new employer through the turnstile, which was swung round obligingly by the other attendant, down a narrow white-washed tunnel into a large apartment.

'Ever seen figures before?' inquired Mr Mugivan.

'Waxworks? Not since I was a kid.'

'Hall of Monarchs,' said Mr Mugivan, sucking his teeth with a deprecating sound.

The room in which they found themselves was bare and vault-like; here, too, the walls were white-washed; the floor was covered with a red drugger, and in the middle of the room was placed a sofa upholstered in shabby crimson plush. Yet although bare the room was not empty, but crowded, crowded with a pale throng of mute and stiff and silent figures. They stood in groups, a dais to each group, and were protected from the public by a red cord which imprisoned them, like sheep in a pen, so that had they wished they could not have strayed, but must forever remain captive. There they stood and would no doubt stand throughout the ages, these tinsel kings and queens, Plantagenets and Stuarts, Tudors and Hanoverians, calm and blank and dreadfully remote, pallid of cheek and glassy of eye, indifferent to all who passed by to gape at them—a host of waxen princes, all dead, many of them forgotten, terribly isolated in their garish splendour, uncannily galvanized into a crude semblance of life that yet denied them even the elements of life, leaving them fixed, frozen and staring, while the dust thickened upon their cheap and fusty robes of purple and sham ermine.

Opposite the door through which they had come was another door leading to yet another chamber. Mr Mugivan led the way.

'Curiosities and Horrors,' he explained carelessly. They passed through the second door.

Here was another room, replica of the first, but more dimly lit, more melancholy than even the Hall of Monarchs, since the illumination that winked upon this dreary scene was greenish, ghastly, such a light as might have been expected to proceed from a sconce of corpse candles. Here were more massed ranks of still, impassive figures, paler these than the monarchs in the dim grotto of their melancholy chamber, and more repellent perhaps because their stiff, indifferent bodies were clothed in the garments of everyday and borrowed no majesty from princes' robes, however sham. A skeleton gleamed white in one corner of the room, there was a stuffed ox with six legs, a tiny waxen midget and a giant of local fame. Save for these the room was peopled only with men who had killed and who had paid the penalty for killing. A throng staring before them, expressionless, rigid, mask-like, brooding perhaps upon their crimes.

Mr Mugivan seemed more at home in the second room. He became almost conversational.

'Here's Hopkins, the Norwich strangler... Tracey, who shot a policeman John Joseph Gilmore, cut the throats of his wife and two children...'

They moved across the room. Then, near the slit of a window, crossed by iron bars, Patrick saw her for the first time. She stood on a little dais by herself, a young woman, or, rather, the effigy of a young woman, dressed neatly in dark clothes that were already old-fashioned in cut. She carried herself proudly, like a queen, and whereas the other waxworks were completely expressionless of countenance, this one alone, with proudly curling lips and short, imperious nose, seemed, he thought, actually to live, perhaps because she was disdain incarnate. She stood there easily, gracefully, long, pale hands folded upon her breast, and Patrick, gazing, felt the cool, amused stare of her grey eyes. For a moment his heart leaped sharply, startling him, and he had a sudden impulse to move forward and look more closely at her; then this sensation was succeeded by a creeping feeling of curious discomfort. He was embarrassed; he had to avert his eyes.

'Who's that woman?' he asked impetuously, and then wished that he had not spoken. Mr Mugivan answered him casually, with his back turned to the effigy

'That's Mrs Raeburn, the poisoner and that's the lot, so come on.'

'Mrs Raeburn? I seem to know the name.'

'No doubt, no doubt, it was well enough known at one time.'

They walked away, towards the Hall of Monarchs, and

Patrick was acutely conscious of the supercilious grey eyes that must be gazing after them. The sham eyes of a sham woman, a waxen effigy! He felt acutely ridiculous.

Mr Mugivan said no more until they found themselves once again in the little office. Then, offering Patrick a cigarette, he asked suddenly:

'You're not a fanciful sort of chap by any chance?'

'Fanciful? You mean nervous? No, I can't say that I am. Why?'

'No place for fancies, this,' confided Mr Mugivan, waving his hand in the direction of the exhibition; 'it's a lonely sort of a job most of the time, and once you start thinking the figures are looking at you, well, you're done, that's all. Last chap we had here took to having fancies. That's why you've got his job.'

Patrick felt suddenly rebellious.

'I can safely say I shan't have fancies,' he said, laughing. 'I may not be particularly brave—in fact I'm not—but I must say it would take more than a parcel of wax dolls to scare me.'

'Figures aren't dolls,' Mr Mugivan corrected, shocked.

'Figures, then,' and he thought: 'Talking of figures, that woman Mrs Raeburn's got a good one.'

But neither he nor Mr Mugivan mentioned the name of the woman poisoner aloud.

'Nine o'clock tomorrow, then,' said Mr Mugivan.

'Nine o'clock tomorrow.'

And so they parted.

He discovered, the next day, two things about his new job. One was that his long and often lonely vigil with the waxworks gave him at times the curious and eerie sensation of being buried alive in a vault filled with the dead, the other that, with the morning, Mrs Raeburn, poisoner, had become once more a waxen effigy; and was no longer a living, breathing woman.

This was comforting, yet in some strange way disappointing, for it was idle to deny that he had thought of her very frequently during the course of the night, and that the prospect of meeting once more the direct gaze of her rather mocking eyes had undoubtedly stimulated him and sent him forth into the cheerless streets kindled with an eager, sparkling excitement which he rather half-heartedly strove to suppress.

As the morning dragged by he studied a catalogue of the exhibition, trying to memorize the many dossiers of princes and murderers. He was accustomed to learn by heart, and in three hours his task was almost complete, yet with one exception. A curious revulsion prevented him from reading, even to himself, the brief account in the catalogue of Mrs Raeburn's crime, of discovering, through the medium of one cheap, smudged paragraph, that she had been an infamous woman, a monster of vice and cruelty. Taking a pen-knife from his pocket he cut away from his catalogue all record of her dark deeds. Yet she remained throughout the morning a lifeless effigy, and after glancing at her once, he gladly looked away.

He went out to lunch and returned for the long vigil of the afternoon. Few people came to visit the exhibition: a pair of schoolchildren in charge of a maiden aunt, two girls, who giggled and eyed him coyly, an old man, and an amorous couple who plainly regarded his presence as a nuisance.

It was foggy outside; dusk fell early for the first time that day, as he paced the Hall of Monarchs, he became sensible of the loneliness of his position. Once again the feeling of being buried among the dead returned to him, intensified this time by a bored and brooding melancholy, whereas in the morning there had also been a sense of adventure. The very tread of his feet, the only sound in the still apartment, smote lugubriously upon his ears. He would have liked to smoke, but this was, of course, forbidden.

At length he turned, and obeying an impulse which was becoming every second stronger, he moved towards the farther chamber, the Hall of Curiosities and Horrors. Here the twilight struck gloomily upon the wan and glimmering faces of the murderers, upturned to greet the first dark, smoky greyness of night: greenish they were once more, and dismal; and very hopeless in the blank resignation of their weary vigil in this dim room that was filled with the very breath of genteel decay.

He went straight towards the figure of Mrs Raeburn, standing tall and quiet and erect on her dais below the baited window. He had never been so near to her before; their eyes met, and once more she had recaptured that spark of life which had so curiously impressed him on the previous day. He gazed for some moments at her pale, clear-cut face, at her direct, ironic eyes. She appeared to return his scrutiny gravely, earnestly, scornfully, yet with glint of interest and humour in her regard. She seemed, he thought, a woman well used to curious eyes, well able to defend herself against the stares of the inquisitive. Suddenly to his immense astonishment, he spoke to her, and his voice rang out strangely enough in that silent room.

'I wonder what you have done?' he asked her abruptly. 'For God's sake, what can you have done that you should be here?'

There was a long pause, during the course of which he continued to examine her closely. Was it his imagination, or did her lips really curve, was there an answering twinkle in her eye? And then he turned sharply, for he had caught, or thought that he had caught, a soft, eager rustling sound from the throng of effigies behind his back. And suddenly he was saved, for two little boys came pattering in to visit the curiosities and horrors.

The next day saw him resolutely keeping to the Hall of Monarchs. Here, with the lifeless dummies of long dead kings, he was safe. In that other room he realized that he was in peril. And the day after, although he hungered for a glimpse of Mrs Raeburn's pale face, he still remained aloof. The next day was Saturday, with a steady stream of patrons who would have made the dankest vault seem homely and prosaic. Then Sunday, a holiday.

On Monday he returned to the exhibition ready to laugh at himself for a morbid fool. The rain had stopped; a feeble ray of primrose sunshine, filtering through the barred window of the second chamber, made even Mrs Raeburn seem little more than a cunningly fashioned doll of life size. And he had spoken to her, as though she were alive and could hear and understand him! He was disgusted with himself.

Yet, with the swiftly flowing dusk the murderers changed once more; assumed as was their wont with the shades of night the vivid and evil personalities they must have worn during their lifetime; seemed to stretch themselves as though released from some long spell of immobility; nodded, perhaps, to one another—even winked; perhaps brushed the dust from their shabby garments, smothered yawns, and waited, quietly expectant, for the closing of the exhibition. So Patrick thought, but it was difficult to see, for the shadows were thick in this lost and forgotten room.

He went towards the effigy of Mrs Raeburn and was not surprised to find that her eyes, alive and brilliant, almost feverish in their eager intensity; remained fixed direct upon him as though she waited to see whether he would, after his three days' absence, speak once more to her.

He was, however silent. He stared at her proud and beautiful mouth, at her long, pale hands, at the white stem of her throat, and admitted to himself that he desired her. Yet he had no immediate wish to touch her, but only longed passionately for the stiff, waxen body of this effigy to melt and transform itself into warm living flesh and blood. Somewhere, somehow, this miracle must be accomplished, for he was unable to possess her he thought that, such was the spell she had cast upon him, he must inevitably pine and sicken, for she was La Belle Dame Sans Merci, and he was in her thrall. At last he spoke to her, softly, scarcely knowing that he spoke.

'You are a witch,' he said, 'and you possess me body and soul. You ought to be burnt, and since you are made of wax it should not be difficult to destroy you... I have a good mind to try.'

This time there was no mistake; a gleam of sardonic laughter came to her eyes, a strange and elfin smile to her curling lips. She defied him. And as before, the tow of murderers behind seemed to move simultaneously with the rustling murmur of excitement. As before, too, he was saved by a footstep from the outer world. He turned sharply. A woman came into the room.

Patrick stiffened, became once more the respectful and vigilant attendant. The woman hesitated for a moment, then approached him slowly, for she was bent and squat and elderly, and walked with the help of a stick. He noticed vaguely that she was dressed in dingy black, with a frowsy bonnet askew upon her head and a film of veil that partially concealed her face. He bent down politely.

'Yes, madam? Is there anything I can do?'

'There is,' said the old woman. Her voice was clear and decisive, the voice of one who is accustomed to command. 'I have stupidly neglected to buy a catalogue at the door, and as I am old, and not so good a walker as I was, I wonder if you would save my going back by being kind enough to tell me something about the waxworks. These are murderers, are they not?'

Patrick, only too pleased to occupy his mind in this accustomed fashion, began mechanically:

'Yes, madam. There on my right is Richard Sayers, the Scottish body-snatcher, who shot two men before he was arrested, and protested his innocence to the last... Next to Sayers is Mugivan's conception of Jack the Ripper, the criminal who was never captured...this figure is modelled according to the description of his appearance given to the police by those persons who protested that they had seen him before or after his appalling crimes... Next to Jack the Ripper we have Landru...'

But while his voice droned on he was dreading the moment when they must face Mrs Raeburn, when he would look once more upon her pale, remote face and meet once again her steady, contemptuous gaze. He lingered beside the midget, the freakish ox, the local giant. The old woman listened to him attentively, beady eyes darting from beneath her heavy veil. Once or twice she asked him a question but otherwise was silent, seeming pleasantly absorbed in his monotonous catalogue of grim and fiendish crimes. At last the moment dreaded by Patrick could be postponed no longer; at last they faced the figure of Mrs Raeburn, standing slim and straight and self-possessed beneath the grating window. Suddenly Patrick remembered that he knew nothing of this murderess save that she had killed by poison; here he was speechless and could recite no bloodthirsty dossier, nor did he even know her victim; only that she was young and fair and that she had cast a spell upon him, and these things could not be told to his companion. There was a pause during the course of which the old woman examined the wax figure attentively and in silence. At length he mumbled:

'This is Mrs Raeburn the poisoner.'

As he spoke he shot a sharp glance at the effigy and observed that she was blank and mask-like once more; indifferent both to him and his companion. His witch had again become a waxwork.

The old lady shuffled closer to the figure, peered with a certain attentive inquisitiveness, then turned to him and remarked critically:

'The likeness is not very good.'

He was startled, and gaped, unable quite to grasp the purport of her words.

He asked, 'You knew her?'

She did not answer him, but said, still peering: 'She was taller, she had more dignity, more of an air. And I think she was wilder. But it's long ago,' and her face changed all the time.

He asked again, trembling, his hands clammy cold, his voice unconsciously menacing: 'You knew her?'

For the first time the old creature turned to look at him, seeming to observe him closely. She chuckled, and at first he thought that one of the waxworks had laughed, so ghostly, so unexpected, was this little bubbling sound in the quietness of the dim hall.

She said, still chuckling: 'I am Mrs Raeburn.'

And as he did not answer she pulled back her veil. She was younger than he had at first supposed. She revealed a fat, gross, heavy-jowled face, sallow, unhealthy, with high Mongolian cheekbones. Her nose was squat and thick, her cheeks carved with two deep-cut lines running from her nostrils to the corners of her mouth. Her little sharp grey eyes were almost buried in folds of flesh. Beneath the shoddy bonnet a strand of hair hung untidily; it was dyed a bright orange tint. The face, which leered forth so boldly at Patrick, was seamed and stamped with the marks of every foul and obscene vice; brazen, debauched, so brutal as to be three parts animal, it seemed to hang in the air, this gargoyle face, to gloat triumphantly upon his horror and confusion. Then, swiftly, the woman whisked back her veil and said crisply, in her clear and resonant voice:

'It didn't do me justice, your image.' Then in a moment she was gone, while behind her the effigy of Mrs Raeburn, poisoner, remained standing cool and pale and remote upon her dais, all the paler, all the cooler, for being now the centre of a flood of cold and frozen moonlight.

Patrick fled after the old woman, not because he wished to see her again, but because of the two of them the waxen image had become the more repulsive, yet, when he reached the Hall of Monarchs, she had already disappeared.

He waited, sick and shivering, until the clock struck seven and the show shut down, then he went in search of Mr Mugivan, whom he found in his office, reading an evening paper, with his feet on his desk.

'Good evening,' said Patrick. 'I want to tell you something.' Mr Mugivan put down his paper.

'My word, young fellow, you look cheap. What is it now?'

Patrick, gulping, said, 'Do you know who's been here this afternoon?'

'I do not,' said Mr Mugivan. 'I'm proprietor of a waxwork show, not a magician. Who has been here?'

'Mrs Raeburn. The real Mrs Raeburn. She came to see her waxwork. She's just gone.'

As Mr Mugivan gaped, his red face became curiously mottled-white and purple in patches, Patrick noticed dispassionately.

'Mrs Raeburn?'

'Yes.'

Mr Mugivan climbed laboriously from his chair.

'Mrs Raeburn, eh? Somebody's been pulling your leg. You don't know your catalogue, either. Mrs Raeburn indeed?'

And he pulled a document from the untidy desk, licked his thumb, and flipped over a page.

'Mrs Raeburn,' he said, speaking very loud and not looking at Patrick, 'was scragged—hanged, you understand—hanged by the neck for the murder of her husband more than twenty years ago. That being so, you could hardly have seen her here just now. And that's enough of your funny stuff for one day.'

Patrick said nothing. There was really nothing to say nor did Mr Mugivan break the silence, but waddled to and fro about the little room, changing his carpet slippers for boots, struggling into his overcoat, cramming a check cap upon his head. In a moment he was gone.

Patrick switched off the office light, then went forth, as was his custom, to extinguish the gas jets in the exhibition before locking up for the night. His comrade of the turnstile had already gone home; he was alone, entirely alone, with more than a hundred waxen effigies. It was now quite dark outside, for the moon had fled behind a screen of clouds, and there was a rushing sound of strong wind, which swept in gusts past the shuttered windows.

He paused to light a forbidden cigarette, and then it was that he realized with an odd detachment that what he had seen during the afternoon was not a ghost, but something even more monstrous—a disembodied soul. The foul and evil soul of this wretched woman whose lovely image had bewitched him. The hideous reflection of a hideous mind. Behind her seeming purity and beauty had always been this horror, dormant, waiting to leap forth and devour. The wind rose, moaning, battering at the panes.

On such a night, he mused, as he tramped towards the monarchs, ghouls would surely stalk abroad and witches soar through the air clutching their broomsticles and screaming aloud their lust for Satan. Vampires, sorcerers, fiends. A nightmare pack of horrors... He stretched on tip-toe to lower the gas above the wan, impassive face of King Richard II... And in the old days witches were burnt alive like the guys now consumed by flames each Fifth of November... And after burning he supposed that these evil women could do no more harm, but were destroyed forever, they and their spells. A good job, too. He entered the second chamber.

◆

That night the inhabitants of the city were surprised to perceive a crimson flush sweeping the sky above the roof-tops of a distant street. Then came a clanging of bells, a roar of motor-engines, and, hot-foot, in pursuit of the fire brigade, a yelling, excited rabble. Mugivan's Waxwork Exhibition was on fire. No one wanted to miss the show, doubly welcome because it was free.

The wind was strong that night, and licked the flames eagerly, strengthening them until the efforts of the men armed with hose-pipes became pathetic in their futility At length the roof crashed in, and a wall of roaring flame rose as though to leap into the sky. They were triumphant, these pillars of fire, as though they knew that they were purifying, destroying a witch. By morning Mugivan's Waxwork Show was a drenched and a sooty ruin. Many of the figures were entirely destroyed, the monarchs having been on the whole unluckier than the murderers. Down in the Hall of Curiosities and Horrors there were a few survivors. Some were quite untouched. Mrs Raeburn, for instance, appeared to have emerged unscathed from the ordeal, and stood upon her dais proudly and gracefully, pale hands folded demurely upon her breast. And yet, on closer inspection, Mrs Raeburn proved not to be entirely unharmed. Her waxen face had melted, and running, the stuff had twisted upon her features a strange and devilish sneer. Save for her pride of carriage she was unrecognizable, distorted. And then the firemen made a further discovery.

Lying near by, where the flames had crackled most fiercely, was a charred and sodden bundle of clothing. They bent to examine it. It was, they found, a human body, the body of a young man.

THE VAMPIRE

Sydney Horler

Until his death, quite recently, I used to visit at least once a week a Roman Catholic priest. The fact that I am a Protestant did nothing to shake our friendship. Father R—was one of the finest characters I have ever known; he was capable of the broadest sympathies, and was, in the best sense of that frequently-abused term, 'a man of the world.' He was good enough to take considerable interest in my work as a novelist, and I often discussed plots and situations with him.

The story I am about to relate occurred about eighteen months ago-ten months before his illness. I was then writing my novel *The Curse of Doone*. In this story I made the villain take advantage of a ghasty legend attached to an old manor-house in Devonshire and use it for his own ends.

Father R—listened while I outlined the plot I had in mind, and then said, to my great surprise: 'Certain people may scoff because they will not allow themselves to believe that there is any credence in the vampire tradition.'

'Yes, that is so,' I parried; 'but, all the same, Bram Stoker stirred the public imagination with his "Dracula"—one of the most horrible and yet fascinating books ever written and I am hoping that my public will extend to me the customary "author's licence."'

My friend nodded.

'Quite,' he replied. 'As a matter of fact,' he went on to say, 'I believe in vampires myself.'

'You do?' I felt the hair on the back of my neck commence to irritate. It is one thing to write about a horror, but quite another to begin to see it assume definite shape. 'Yes,' said Father R—'I am forced to believe in vampires for the very good but terrible reason that I have met one!'

I half-rose in my chair. There could be no questioning R—'s word, and yet—

'That, no doubt, my dear fellow,' he continued, 'may appear a very extraordinary statement to have made, and yet I assure you it is the truth. It happened many years ago and in another part of the country—exactly where I do not think I had better tell you.'

'But this is amazing—you say you actually met a vampire face to face?'

'And talked to him. Until now I have never mentioned the matter to a living soul apart from a brother priest.'

It was clearly an invitation to listen; I crammed tobacco into my pipe and leaned back in the chair on the opposite side of the crackling fire. I had heard that truth was said to be stranger than fiction—but here I was about to have, it seemed, the strange experience of listening to my own most sensational imagining being hopelessly out-done by *fact!*

'The name of the small town does not matter' (Father R— started); 'let it suffice it was in the West of England and was inhabited by a good many people of superior means. There was a large city seventy-five miles away and business men, when they retired, often came to—to wind up their lives. I was young and very happy there in my work until—but I am a little previous.

'I was on very friendly terms with a local doctor; he often used to come in and have a chat when he could spare the time. We used to try to thresh out many problems which later experience has convinced me are insoluble in this world, at least.

'One night, he looked at me rather curiously, I thought.'

'"What do you think of that man, Farington?" he asked.

'Now, it was a curious fact that he should have made that inquiry at that exact moment, for by some subconscious means I happened to be thinking of this very person myself.

'The man who called himself "Joseph Farington" was a stranger who had recently come to settle in—. That circumstance alone would have caused comment, but when I say that he had bought the largest house on the hill overlooking the town on the south side (representing the best residential quarter) and had it furnished apparently regardless of cost by one of the famous London houses, that he sought to entertain a great deal but that no one seemed anxious to go twice to "The Gables."—Well, there was "something funny" about Farington, it was whispered.

'I knew this, of course—the smallest fragment of gossip comes to a priest's ear—and so I hesitated before replying to the doctor's direct question.

'"Confess now, Father," said my companion, "you are like all the rest of us—you don't like the man! He has made me his medical attendant, but I wish to goodness he had chosen someone else. There's 'something funny' about him."

'"Something funny"—there it was again. As the doctor's words sounded in my ears I remembered Farington as I had last seen him walking up the main street with every other eye half-turned in his direction. He was a big-framed man, the essence of masculinity. He looked so robust that the thought came instinctively: This man will never die. He had a florid complexion; he walked with the elasticity of youth and his hair was jet-black. Yet from remarks he had made the impression in—was that Farington must be at least sixty years of age.

"'Well, there's one thing, Sanders," I replied; "if appearances are anything to go by, Farington will not be giving you much trouble. The fellow looks as strong as an ox.'"

"'You haven't answered my question," persisted the doctor. "Forget your cloth, Father, and tell me exactly what you think of Joseph Farington. Don't you agree that he is a man to give you the shudders?'"

"'You—a doctor—talking about getting the shudders!'" I gently scoffed because I did not want to give my real opinion of Joseph Farington.

"'I can't help it—I have an instinctive horror of the fellow. This afternoon I was called up to 'The Gables'. Farington, like ever so many of his ox-like kind, is really a bit of a hypochondriac. He thought there was something wrong with his heart, he said.'"

"'And was there?'"

"'The man ought to live to a hundred! But, I tell you, Father, I hated having to be near the fellow, there's something uncanny about him. I felt frightened—yes, frightened—all the time I was in the house. I had to talk to someone about it and as you are the safest person in—I dropped in… You haven't said anything yourself, I notice.'"

"'I prefer to wait," I replied. It seemed the safest answer.

'Two months after that conversation with Sanders, not only— but the whole of the country was startled and horrified by a terrible crime. A girl of eighteen, the belle of the district, was found dead in a field. Her face, in life so beautiful, was revolting in death because of the expression of dreadful horror it held.

'The poor girl had been murdered—but in a manner which sent shudders of fear racing up and down people's spines... There was a great hole in the throat, as though a beast of the jungle had attacked...

'It is not difficult to say how suspicion for this fiendish crime first started to fasten itself on Joseph Farington, preposterous as the statement may seem. Although he had gone out of his way to become sociable, the man had made no real friends. Sanders, although a clever doctor, was not the most tactful of men and there is no doubt that his refusal to visit Farington professionally— he had hinted as much on the night of his visit to me, you will remember—got noised about. In any case, public opinion was strongly roused; without a shred of direct evidence to go upon, people began to talk of Farington as being the actual murderer. There was some talk among the wild young spirits of setting fire to "The Gables" one night, and burning Farington in his bed.

'It was whilst this feeling was at its height that, very unwillingly, as you may imagine, I was brought into the affair. I received a note from Farington asking me to dine with him one night.

"I have something on my mind which I wish to talk over with you; so please do not fail me."

'These were the concluding words of the letter.

'Such an appeal could not be ignored by a man of religion and so I replied accepting.

'Farington was a good host; the food was excellent; on the surface there was nothing wrong. But—and here is the curious part—from the moment I faced the man I knew there was something wrong. I had the same uneasiness as Sanders, the doctor: *I felt afraid.* The man had an aura of evil; he was possessed of some devilish force or quality which chilled me to the marrow.

'I did my best to hide my discomfiture, but when, after dinner, Farington began to speak about the murder of that poor, innocent girl, this feeling increased. And at once the terrible truth leaped into my mind: I knew it was Farington who had done this crime: the man was a monster!

'Calling upon all my strength, I challenged him.

'"You wished to see me tonight for the purpose of easing your soul of a terrible burden," I said; "you cannot deny that it was you who killed that unfortunate girl."

'"Yes," he replied slowly, 'that is the truth. I killed the girl. The demon which possesses me forced me to do it. But you, as a priest, must hold this confession sacred—you must preserve it as a secret. Give me a few more hours; then I will decide myself what to do.'

'I left shortly afterwards. The man would not say anything more.

'Give me a few hours,' he repeated.

'That night I had a horrible dream. I felt I was suffocating. Scarcely able to breathe, I rushed to the window, pulled it open and then fell senseless to the floor. The next thing I remember was Dr Sanders—who had been summoned by my faithful housekeeper—bending over me.

'"What happened?" he asked. "You had a look on your face as though you had been staring into hell.'

'"So I had," I replied.

'"Had it anything to do with Farington?" he asked bluntly.

'"Sanders," and I clutched him by the arm in the intensity

of my feeling, 'does such a monstrosity as a vampire exist nowadays? Tell me, I implore you!'

'The good fellow forced me to take another sip of brandy before he would reply.

'Then he put a question himself. "Why do you ask that?" he said.

'"It sounds incredible—and I hope I really dreamed it—but I fainted tonight because I saw—or imagined I saw—the man Farington flying past the window that I had just opened.'

'"I am not surprised," he nodded. "Ever since I examined the mutilated body of that poor girl I came to the conclusion that she had come to her death through some terrible abnormality."

'"Although we hear practically nothing about vampirism nowadays,' he continued, 'that is not to say that ghoulish spirits do not still take up their abode in a living man or woman, thus conferring upon them supernatural powers. What form was the shape you thought you saw?"

'"It was like a huge bat," I replied shuddering.

'"Tomorrow," said Sanders determinedly, "I'm going to London to see Scotland Yard. They may laugh at me at first, but—"

'Scotland Yard did not laugh. But criminals with supernatural powers were rather out of their line, and, besides, as they told Sanders, they had to have proof before they could convict Farington. Even my testimony—had I dared to break my priestly pledge, which, of course, I couldn't in any circumstances do would not have been sufficient.

'Farington solved the terrible problem by committing suicide. He was found in bed with a bullet wound in his head.

'But, according to Sanders, only the body is dead—the vile spirit is roaming free, looking for another human habitation.

'God help its luckless victim.'

CORONER'S INQUEST

Marc Connelly

'What is your name?'

'Frank Wineguard.'

'Where do you live?'

A hundred and eighty-five West Fifty-fifth Street.'

'What is your business?'

'I'm stage manager for *Hello, America*.'

'You were the employer of James Dawle?'

'In a way. We both worked for Mr Bender, the producer, but I have charge backstage.'

'Did you know Theodore Rebel?'

'Yes, sir.'

'Was he in your company, too?'

'No, sir. I met him when we started rehearsals. That was about three months ago, in June. We sent out a call for midgets and he and Jimmy showed up together, with a lot of others. Robel was too big for us. I didn't see him again until we broke into their room Tuesday.'

'You discovered their bodies?'

'Yes, sir. Mrs Pike, there, was with me.'

'You found them both dead?'

'Yes, sir.'

'How did you happen to be over in Jersey City?'

'Well, I called up his house at curtain time Monday night when I found Jimmy hadn't shown up for the performance. Mrs Pike told me they were both out, and I asked her to have either Jimmy or Robel call me when they came in. Then Mrs Pike called me Tuesday morning and said she tried to get into the room but she'd found the door was bolted. She said all her other roomers were out and she was alone and scared.'

'I'd kind of suspected something might be wrong. So I said to her to wait and I'd come over. Then I took the tube over and got there about noon. Then we went up and I broke down the door.'

'Did you see this knife there?'

'Yes, sir. It was on the floor, about a foot from Jimmy.'

'You say you suspected something was wrong. What do you mean by that?'

'I mean I felt something might have happened to Jimmy. Nothing like this, of course. But I knew he'd been feeling very depressed lately, and I knew Robel wasn't helping to cheer him up any.'

'You mean that they had quarrels?'

'No, sir. They just both had the blues. Robel had them for a long time. Robel was Jimmy's brother-in-law. He'd married Jimmy's sister—she was a midget, too—about five years ago, but she died a year or so later. Jimmy had been living with them and after the sister died, he and Robel took a room in Mrs Pike's house together.'

'How did you learn this?'

'Jimmy and I were pretty friendly at the theatre. He was

a nice little fellow and seemed grateful that I'd given him this job. We'd only needed one midget for an Oriental scene in the second act and the agencies had sent about fifteen. Mr Gehring, the director, told me to pick one of them as he was busy and I picked Jimmy because he was the littlest.

'After I got to know him he told me how glad he was I'd given him the job. He hadn't worked for nearly a year. He wasn't little enough to be a featured midget with circuses or in museums, so he had to take whatever came along. Anyway, we got to be friendly and he used to tell me about his brother-in-law and all.'

'He never suggested that there might be ill-feeling between him and his brother-in-law?'

'No, sir. I don't imagine he'd ever had any words at all with Robel. As a matter of fact, from what I could gather I guess Jimmy had quite a lot of affection for him and he certainly did everything he could to help him. Robel was a lot worse off than Jimmy. Robel hadn't worked for a couple of years and Jimmy practically supported him. He used to tell me how Robel had been sunk ever since he got his late growth.'

'His, what?'

'His late growth. I heard it happens among midgets often, but Jimmy told me about it first. Usually a midget will stay as long as he lives at whatever height he reaches when he's fourteen or fifteen, but every now and then one of them starts growing again just before he's thirty, and he can grow a foot or even more in a couple of years. Then he stops growing for good. But, of course, he don't look so much like a midget any more.'

'That's what had happened to Robel about three years ago. Of course he had trouble getting jobs and it hit him pretty hard.

'From what Jimmy told me and from what Mrs Pike says, I

guess he used to talk about it all the time. Robel used to come over and see his agent in New York twice a week, but there was never anything for him. Then he'd go back to Jersey City. Most of the week he lived alone because after the show started Jimmy often stayed in New York with a cousin or somebody that lived uptown.

'Lately Robel hadn't been coming over to New York at all. But every Saturday night Jimmy would go over to Jersey City and stay till Monday with him, trying to cheer him up. Every Sunday they'd take a walk and go to a movie. I guess as they walked along the street Robel realized most the difference in their heights. And I guess that's really why they're both dead now.'

'How do you mean?'

'Well, as I told you, Jimmy would try to sympathize with Robel and cheer him up. He and Robel both realized that Jimmy was working and supporting them and that Jimmy would probably keep right on working, according to the ordinary breaks of the game, while Robel would always be too big. It simply preyed on Robel's mind.

'And then three weeks ago on a Monday Jimmy thought he saw the axe fall.

'I was standing outside the stage door—it was about seven-thirty—and Jimmy came down the alley. He looked down in the mouth, which I thought was strange, seeing that he usually used to come in swinging his little cane and looking pretty cheerful. I said, "How are you feeling, Jimmy?" and he said, "I don't feel so good, Mr Wineguard." So I said, "Why, what's the matter, Jimmy?" I could see there really was something the matter with him by this time.

'"I'm getting scared," he said, and I said, "Why?"

'"I'm starting to grow again," he says. He said it the way you just found out you had some disease that was going to kill you in a week. He looked like he was shivering.

'"Why, you're crazy, Jimmy," I says. "You ain't growing."

'"Yes, I am," he says. "I'm thrity-one and it's that late growth like my brother-in-law has. My father had it, but his people had money, so it didn't make much difference to him. It's different with me. I've got to keep working."

'He went on like that for a while and then I tried to kid him out of it.

'"You look all right to me," I said. "How tall have you been all along?"

'"Thirty-seven inches," he says. So I says, "Come on into the prop-room and I'll measure you."

'He backed away from me. "No," he says, "I don't want to know how much it is." Then he went up to the dressing-room before I could argue with him.

'All week he looked awful sunk. When he showed up the next Monday evening he looked almost white.

'I grabbed him as he was starting upstairs to make-up.

'"Come on out of it," I says. I thought he'd make a break and try to get away from me, but he didn't. He just sort of smiled as if I didn't understand. Finally, he says, "It ain't any use, Mr Wineguard."

'"Listen," I says, "you've been over with that brother-in-law of yours, haven't you?" he said yes, he had. "Well," I says, "that's what's bothering you. From what you tell me about him he's talked about his own tough luck so much that he's given you the willies, too. Stay away from him the end of this week."

'He stood there for a second without saying anything. They he says, "That wouldn't do any good. He's all alone over there and he needs company. Anyway, it's all up with me, I guess. I've grown nearly two inches already."

'I looked at him. He was pretty pathetic, but outside of that there wasn't any change in him as far as I could see.

'I says, "Have you been measured?" he said he hadn't. Then I said, "Then how do you know? Your clothes fit you all right, except your pants, and as a matter of fact they seem a little longer."

'"I fixed my suspenders and let them down a lot farther," he says. "Besides they were always a little big for me."

'"Let's make sure," I says. "I'll get a yardstick and we'll make absolutely sure."

'But I guess he was too scared to face things. He wouldn't do it.

'He managed to dodge me all week. Then, last Saturday night, I ran into him as I was leaving the theatre. I asked him if he felt any better.

'"I feel all right," he says. He really looked scared to death.

'That's the last time I saw him before I went over to Jersey City after Mrs Pike phoned me Tuseday morning.'

'Patrolman Gorlitz has testified that the bodies were in opposite ends of the room when he arrived. They were in that position when you forced open the door?'

'Yes, sir.'

'The medical examiner has testified that they were both dead of knife wounds, apparently from the same knife. Would you assume the knife had fallen from Dawle's hand as he fell?'

'Yes, sir.'

'Has it been your purpose to suggest that both men were driven to despondency by a fear of lack of employment for Dawle, and that they might have committed suicide?'

'No, sir. I don't think anything of the kind.'

'What do you mean?'

'Well, when Mrs Pike and I went in the room and I got a look at the knife, I said to Mrs Pike that that was a funny kind of a knife for them to have in the room. You can see it's a kind a butcher knife. Then Mrs Pike told me it was one that she'd missed from her kitchen a few weeks before. She'd never thought either Robel or Jimmy had stolen it, too. Then I put two and two together and found out what really happened. Have you got the little broken cane that was lying on the bed?'

'Is this it?'

'Yes, sir. Well, I'd never been convinced by Jimmy that he was really growing. So when Mrs Pike told me about the knife I started figuring. I figured that about five minutes before that knife came into play Jimmy must have found it, probably by accident.'

'Why by accident?'

'Because Robel had gone a little crazy, I guess. He'd stolen it and kept it hidden from Jimmy. And when Jimmy found it he wondered what Robel had been doing with it. Then Robel wouldn't tell him and Jimmy found out for himself. Or maybe Robel did tell him. Anyway, Jimmy looked at the cane. It was the one he always carried. He saw where, when Jimmy wasn't looking, Robel had been cutting little pieces off the end of it.

THE STORY OF THE SPANIARDS, HAMMERSMITH

E. and H. Heron

Lieutenant Roderick Houston, of H.M.S. *Sphinx*, had practically nothing beyond his pay, and he was beginning to be very tired of the West African station, when he received the pleasant intelligence that a relative had left him a legacy. This consisted of a satisfactory sum in ready money and a house in Hammersmith, which was rated at over £200 a year, and was said in addition to be comfortably furnished. Houston, therefore, counted on its rental to bring his income up to a fairly desirable figure. Further information from home, however, showed him that he had been rather premature in his expectations, whereupon, being a man of action, he applied for two months' leave, and came home to look after his affairs himself.

When he had been a week in London, he arrived at the conclusion that he could not possibly hope, single-handed, to tackle the difficulties which presented themselves. He accordingly wrote the following letter to his friend, Flaxman Low:

The Spaniards, Hammersmith, 23-3-1892

Dear Low,—Since we parted some three years ago, I have heard very little of you. It was only yesterday that I met our mutual friend, Sammy Smith ('Silkworm' of our schooldays), who told me that your studies have developed in a new direction, and that you are now a good deal interested in psychical subjects. If this be so, I hope to induce you to come and stay with me here for a few days by promising to introduce you to a problem in your own line. I am just now living at 'The Spaniards', a house that has lately been left to me, and which in the first instance was built by an old fellow named Van Nuysen, who married a great-aunt of mine. It is a good house, but there is said to be 'something wrong' with it. It lets easily, but unluckily the tenants cannot be persuaded to remain above a week or two. They complain that the place is haunted by something—presumably a ghost—because its vagaries bear just that brand of inconsequence which stamps the common run of manifestations.

It occurs to me that you may care to investigate the matter with me. If so, send me a wire when to expect you.

Yours ever,
Roderick Houston

Houston waited in some anxiety for an answer. Low was the sort of man one could rely on in almost any emergency. Sammy Smith had told him a characteristic anecdote of Low's career at Oxford, where, although his intellectual triumphs may be forgotten, he will always be remembered by the story that when Sands, of Queen's, fell ill on the day before the Varsity sports, a telegram was sent to Low's rooms: 'Sands ill. You must do the hammer for us.' Low's reply was pithy: 'I'll be there.' Thereupon he finished the treatise upon which he was engaged, and the next day his strong, lean figure was to be seen swinging the hammer amidst vociferous cheering, for that was the occasion on which he not only won the event, but beat the record.

On the fifth day Low's answer came from Vienna. As he read it, Houston recalled the high forehead, long neck—with its accompanying low collar—and thin moustache of his scholarly, athletic friend and smiled. There was so much more in Flaxman Low than anyone gave him credit for.

> My Dear Houston,—Very glad to hear of you again. In response to your kind invitation, I thank you for the opportunity of meeting the ghost, and still more for the pleasure of your companionship. I came here to inquire into a somewhat similar affair. I hope, however, to be able to leave tomorrow, and will be with you some time on Friday evening.
>
> Very sincerely yours,
> Flaxman Low.
>
> P.S.—By the way, will it be convenient to give your servants a holiday during the term of my visit, as, if my investigations are to be of any value, not a grain of dust must be disturbed in your house, excepting by ourselves? —F.L.

'The Spaniards' was within some fifteen minutes' walk of Hammersmith Bridge. Set in the midst of a fairly respectable neighbourhood, it presented an odd contrast to the commonplace dullness of the narrow streets crowded about it. As Flaxman Low drove up in the evening light, he reflected that the house might have come from the back of beyond—it gave an impression of something old-world and something exotic.

It was surrounded by a ten-foot wall, above which the upper storey was visible, and Low decided that this intensely English house still gave some curious suggestion of the tropics. The interior of the house carried out the same idea, with its sense of space and air, cool tints and wide, matted passages.

'So you have seen something yourself since you came?' Low said, as they sat at dinner, for Houston had arranged that meals should be sent in for them from a hotel.

'I've heard tapping up and down the passage upstairs. It is an uncarpeted landing which runs the whole length of the house. One night, when I was quicker than usual, I saw what looked like a bladder disappear into one of the bedrooms—your room it is to be, by the way—and the door closed behind it,' replied Houston discontentedly. 'The usual meaningless antics of a ghost.'

'What had the tenants who lived here to say about it?' went on Low.

'Most of the people saw and heard just what I have told you, and promptly went away. The only one who stood out for a little while was old Filderg—you know the man? Twenty years ago he made an effort to cross the Australian deserts—he stopped for eight weeks. When he left he saw the house-agent, and said he was afraid he had done a little shooting practice in the upper passage, and he hoped it wouldn't count against him in the bill, as it was done in defence of his life. He said something had jumped on to the bed and tried to strangle him. He described it as cold and glutinous, and he pursued it down the passage, firing at it. He advised the owner to have the house pulled down; but, of course, my cousin did nothing of the kind. It's a very good house, and he did not see the sense of spoiling his property.'

'That's very true,' replied Flaxman Low, looking round. 'Mr Van Nuysen had been in the West Indies, and kept his liking for spacious rooms.'

'Where did you hear anything about him?' asked Houston in surprise.

'I have heard nothing beyond what you told me in your letter; but I see a couple of bottles of Gulf weed and a lace-plant ornament, such as people used to bring from the West Indies in former days.'

'Perhaps I should tell you the history of the old man,' said Houston doubtfully; 'but we aren't proud of it!'

Flaxman Low considered a moment.

'When was the ghost seen for the first time?'

'When the first tenant took the house. It was let after old Van Nuysen's time.'

'Then it may clear the way if you will tell me something of him.'

'He owned sugar plantations in Trinidad, where he passed the greater part of his life, while his wife mostly remained in England—incompatibility of temper it was said. When he came home for good, and built this house they still lived apart, my aunt declaring that nothing on earth would persuade her to return to him. In course of time he became a confirmed invalid, and then insisted on my aunt joining him. She lived here for perhaps a year, when she was found dead in bed one morning—in your room.'

'What caused her death?'

'She had been in the habit of taking narcotics, and it was supposed that she smothered herself while under their influence.'

'That doesn't sound very satisfactory,' remarked Flaxman Low. 'Her husband was satisfied with it anyhow, and it was no one else's business. The family were only too glad to have the affair hushed up.'

'And what became of Mr Van Nuysen?'

'That I can't tell you. He disappeared a short time after. Search was made for him in the usual way, but nobody knows to this day what became of him.'

'Ah, that was strange, as he was such an invalid,' said Low, and straightway fell into a long fit of abstraction, from which he was roused by hearing Houston curse the incurable foolishness and imbecility of ghostly behaviour. Flaxman woke up at this. He broke a walnut thoughtfully and began in a gentle voice: 'My dear fellow, we are apt to be hasty in our condemnation of the general behaviour of ghosts. It may appear incalculably foolish in our eyes, and I admit there often seems to be a total absense of any apparent object or intelligent action. But remember that what appears to us to be foolishness may be wisdom in the spirit world, since our unready senses can only catch broken glimpses of what is, I have not the slightest doubt, a coherent whole, if we could trace the connection.'

'There may be something in that,' replied Houston indifferently. 'People naturally say that this ghost is the ghost of old Van Nuysen. But what connection can possibly exist between what I have told you of him and the manifestations—a tapping up and down the passage and the drawing about of a bladder-like a child at play? It sounds idiotic!'

'Certainly. Yet, it need not necessarily be so. There are isolated facts, we must look for the links which lie between. Suppose a saddle and a horseshoe were to be shown to a man who had never seen a horse, I doubt whether he, however intelligent, could evolve the connecting idea! The ways of spirits are strange to us simply because we need further data to help us to interpret them.'

'It's a new point of view,' returned Houston, 'but upon my word, you know, Low, I think you're wasting your time!'

Flaxman Low smiled slowly; his grave, melancholy face brightened.

'I have,' said he, 'gone somewhat deeply into the subject. In other sciences one reasons by analogy. Psychology is unfortunately a science with a future but without a past, or more probably it is a lost science of the ancients. However that may be, we stand today on the frontier of an unknown world, and progress is the result of individual effort; each solution of difficult phenomena forms a step towards the solution of the next problem. In this case, for example, the bladder-like object may be the key to the mystery.'

Houston yawned.

'It all seems pretty senseless, but perhaps you may be able to read reason into it. If it were anything tangible, anything a man could meet with his fists, it would be easier.'

'I entirely agree with you. But suppose we deal with this affair as it stands, on similar lines, I mean on prosaic, rational lines, as we should deal with a purely human mystery.'

'My dear fellow,' returned Houston, pushing his chair back from the table wearily, 'you shall do just as you like, only get rid of the ghost!'

For some time after Low's arrival nothing very special happened. The tappings continued, and more than once Low had been in time to see the bladder disappear into the closing door of his bedroom, though, unluckily, he never chanced to be inside the room on these occasions, and however quickly he followed the bladder, he never succeeded in seeing anything further. He made a thorough examination of the house, and left no space unaccounted for in his careful measurement. There were no cellars, and the foundation of the house consisted of a thick layer of concrete.

At length, on the sixth night, an event took place, which, as Flaxman Low remarked, came very near to putting an end to the investigations as far as he was concerned. For the preceding two nights, he and Houston had kept watch in the hope of getting a glimpse of the person or thing which tapped so persistently up and down the passage. But they were disappointed, for there were no manifestations. On the third evening, therefore, Low went off to his room a little earlier than usual, and fell asleep almost immediately.

He says he was awakened by feeling a heavy weight upon his feet, something that seemed inert and motionless. He recollected that he had left the gas burning, but the room was now in darkness.

Next, he was aware that the thing on the bed had slowly shifted, and was gradually travelling up towards his chest. How it came on the bed he had no idea. Had it leaped or climbed? The sensation he experienced as it moved was of some ponderous, pulpy body, not crawling or creeping, but spreading! It was horrible! He tried to move his lower limbs, but could not because of the deadening weight. A feeling of drowsiness began to overpower him, and a deadly cold, such as he said he had before felt at sea when in the neighbourhood of icebergs, chilled upon the air.

With a violent struggle he managed to free his arms, but the thing grew more irresistible as it spread upwards. Then he became conscious of a pair of glassy eyes, with livid, everted lids, looking into his own. Whether they were human eyes or beast eyes, he could not tell, but they were watery, like the eyes of a dead fish, and gleamed with a pale, internal lustre.

Then he owns he grew afraid. But he was still cool enough to notice one peculiarity about this ghastly visitant—although the head was within a few inches of his own, he could detect no breathing. It dawned upon him that he was about to be suffocated, for, by the same method of extension, the thing was now coming over his face! It felt cold and clammy, like a mass of mucilage or a monstrous snail. And every instant the weight became greater. He is a powerful man, and he struck with his fists again and again at the head. Some substance yielded under the blows with a sickening sensation of bruised flesh.

With a lucky twist he raised himself in the bed and battered away with all the force he was capable of in his cramped position. The only effect was an occasional shudder or quake that ran through the mass as his half-arm blows rained upon it. At last, by chance, his hand knocked against the candle beside him. In a moment he recollected the matches. He seized the box, and struck a light.

As he did so, the lump slid to the floor. He sprang out of bed, and lit the candle. He felt a cold touch upon his leg, but when he looked down there was nothing to be seen. The door, which he had locked overnight, was now open, and he rushed out into the passage. All was still and silent with the throbbing vacancy of night time.

After searching round, he returned to his room. The bed still gave ample proof of the struggle that had taken place, and by his watch he saw the hour to be between two and three.

As there seemed nothing more to be done, he put on his dressing-gown, lit his pipe, and sat down to write an account of the experience he had just passed through for the Psychical Research Society—from which paper the above is an abstract.

He is a man of strong nerves, but he could not disguise from himself that he had been at handgrips with some grotesque form of death. What might be the nature of his assailant he could not determine, but his experience was supported by the attack which had been made on Filderg, and also—it was impossible to avoid the conclusion—by the manner of Mrs Van Nuysen's death.

He thought the whole situation over carefully in connection with the tapping and the disappearing bladder, but, turn these events how he would, he could make nothing of them. They were entirely incongruous. A little later he went and made a shakedown in Houston's room.

'What was the thing!' asked Houston, when Low had ended his story of the encounter.

Low shrugged his shoulders.

'At least, it proves that Filderg did not dream,' he said.

'But this is monstrous! We are more in the dark than ever. There's nothing for it but to have the house pulled down. Let us leave today.'

'Don't be in a hurry, my dear fellow. You would rob me of a very great pleasure; besides, we may be on the verge of some valuable discovery. This series of manifestations is even more interesting than the Vienna mystery I was telling you of.'

'Discovery or not,' replied the other, 'I don't like it.'

The first thing next morning Low went out for a quarter of an hour. Before breakfast a man with a barrowful of sand came into the garden. Low looked up from his paper, leant out of the window, and gave some order.

When Houston came down a few minutes later he saw the

yellowish heap on the lawn with some surprise.

'Hullo! What's this?' he asked.

'I ordered it,' replied Low.

'All right. What's it for?'

'To help us in our investigations. Our visitor is capable of being felt, and he or it left a very distinct impression on the bed. Hence I gather it can also leave an impression on sand. It would be an immense advance if we could arrive at any correct notion of what sort of feet the ghost walks on. I propose to spread a layer of this sand in the upper passage, and the result should be footmarks if the tapping comes tonight.'

That evening the two men made a fire in Houston's bedroom, and sat there smoking and talking, to leave the ghost 'a free run for once', as Houston phrased it. The tapping was heard at the usual hour, and presently the accustomed pause at the other end of the passage and the quiet closing of the door.

Low heaved a long sigh of satisfaction as he listened.

'That's my bedroom door,' he said: 'I know the sound of it perfectly. In the morning, and with the help of daylight, we shall see what we shall see.'

As soon as there was light enough for the purpose of examining the footprints, Low roused Houston.

Houston was as full of excitement as a boy, but his spirits fell by the time he had passed from end to end of the passage.

'There are marks,' he said, 'but they are as perplexing as everything else about this haunting brute, whatever it is. I suppose you think this is the print left by the thing which attacked you the night before last?'

'I fancy it is,' said Low, who was still bending over the floor eagerly. 'What do you make of it, Houston?'

'The brute has only one leg, to start with,' replied Houston, 'and that leaves the mark of a large, clawless pad! It's some animal—some ghoulish monster!'

'On the contrary,' said Low, 'I think we have now every reason to conclude that it is a man?'

'A man? What man ever left footmarks like these?'

'Look at these hollows and streaks at the sides; they are the traces of the sticks we have heard tapping.'

'You don't convince me,' returned Houston doggedly.

'Let us wait another twenty-four hours, and tomorrow night, if nothing further occurs, I will give you my conclusions. Think it over. The tapping, the bladder, and the fact that Mr Van Nuysen had lived in Trinidad. Add to these things this single pad-like print. Does noting strike you by way of a solution?'

Houston shook his head.

'Nothing. And I fail to connect any of these things with what happened both to you and Filderg.'

'Ah! Now,' said Flaxman Low, his face clouding a little, 'I confess you lead me into a somewhat different region, though to me the connection is perfect.'

Houston raised his eyebrows and laughed.

'If you can unravel this tangle of hints and events and diagnose the ghost, I shall be extremely astonished,' he said. 'What can you make of the footless impression?'

'Something, I hope. In fact, that mark may be a clue—an outrageous one, perhaps, but still a clue.'

That evening the weather broke, and by night the storm had risen to a gale, accompanied by sharp bursts of rain.

'It's a noisy night,' remarked Houston; 'I don't suppose we'll hear the ghost, supposing it does turn up.'

This was after dinner, as they were about to go into the

smoking-room. Houston, finding the gas low in the hall, stopped to turn it higher; at the same time asking Low to see if the jet on the upper landing was also alight.

Flaxman Low glanced up and uttered a slight exclamation, which brought Houston to his side.

Looking down at them from over the banisters was a face—a blotched, yellowish face, flanked by two swollen, protruding ears, the whole aspect being strangely leonine. It was but a glimpse, a clash of meeting glances, as it were a glare of defiance, and the face was quickly withdrawn as the two men literally leapt up the stairs.

'There's nothing here,' exclaimed Houston, after a search had been carried out through every room above.

'I didn't suppose we'd find anything,' returned Low.

'This fairly knots up the thread,' said Houston. 'You can't pretend to unravel it now.'

'Come down,' said Low briefly; 'I'm ready to give you my opinion, such as it is.'

Once in the smoking-room, Houston busied himself in turning on all the light he could procure, then he saw to securing the windows, and piled up an immense fire, while Flaxman Low, who, as usual, had a cigarette in his mouth, sat on the edge of the table and watched him with some amusement.

'You saw that abominable face?' cried Houston, as he threw himself into a chair. 'It was as material as yours or mine. But where did he go to? He must be somewhere about.'

'We saw him clearly. That is sufficient for our purpose.'

'You are very good at enumerating points, Low. Now just listen to my list. The difficulties grow with every fresh discovery. We're at a deadlock now, I take it? The sticks and the tapping point to an old man, the playing with a bladder to a child; the footmark might be the pad of a tiger minus claws, yet the thing that attacked you at night was cold and pulpy. And, lastly, by way of a wind-up, we see a lion-like, human face! If you can make all these items square with each other, I'll be happy to hear what you have got to say.'

'You must first allow me to ask you a question. I understood you to say that no blood relationship existed between you and old Mr Van Nuysen?'

'Certainly not. He was quite an outsider,' answered Houston brusquely.

'In that case you are welcome to my conclusions. All the things you have mentioned point to one explanation. This house is haunted by the ghost of Mr Van Nuysen, and he was a leper.'

Houston stood up and stared at his companion.

'What a horrible notion! I must say I fail to see how you have arrived at such a conclusion.'

'Take the chain of evidence in a rather different order,' said Low. 'Why should a man tap with a stick?'

'Generally because he's blind.'

'In cases of blindness, one stick is used for guidance. Here we have two for support.'

'A man who has lost the use of his feet.'

'Exactly; a man who has from some cause partially lost the use of his feet.'

'But the bladder and the lion-like face?' went on Houston.

'The bladder, or what seemed to us to resemble a bladder, was one of his feet, contorted by the disease and probably swathed in linen, which foot he dragged rather than used; consequently, in passing through a door, for example, he would be in the habit of drawing it in after him. Now, as regards the single footmark we saw. In one form of leprosy, the smaller bones of the extremities frequently fall away. The pad-like impression was, as I believe, the mark of the other foot—a toeless foot which he used, because in a more advanced stage of the disease the maimed hand or foot heals and becomes callous.'

'Go on,' said Houston; 'it sounds as if it might be true. And the lion-like face I can account for myself. I have been in China, and have seen it before in lepers.'

'Mr Van Nuysen had been in Trinidad for many years, as we know, and while there he probably contracted the disease.'

'I suppose so. After his return,' added Houston, 'he shut himself up almost entirely, and gave out that he was a martyr to rheumatic gout, this awful thing being the true explanation.'

'It also accounts for Mrs Van Nuysen's determination not to return to her husband.'

Houston appeared much disturbed.

'We can't drop it here, Low,' he said, in a constrained voice. 'There is a good deal more to be cleared up yet. Can you tell me more?'

'From this point I find myself on less certain ground,' replied Low unwillingly. 'I merely offer a suggestion, remember—I don't ask you to accept it. I believe Mrs Van Nuysen was murdered!'

'What?' exclaimed Houston. 'By her husband?'

'Indications tend that way.'

'But, my good fellow—'

'He suffocated her and then made away with himself. It is a pity that his body was not recovered. The condition of the remains would he the only really satisfactory test of my theory. If the skeleton could even now be found, the fact that he was a leper would be finally settled.'

There was a prolonged pause until Houston put another question.

'Wait a minute, Low,' he said. 'Ghosts are admittedly immaterial. In this instance our spook has an extremely palpable body. Surely this is rather unusual? You have made everything else more or less plain. Can you tell me why this dead leper should have tried to murder you and old Filderg? And also how he came to have the actual physical power to do so?'

Low removed his cigarette to look thoughtfully at the end of it. 'Now I lapse into the purely theoretical,' he answered. 'Cases have been known where the assumption of diabolical agency is apparently justifiable.'

'Diabolical agency?—I don't follow you.'

'I will try to make myself clear, though the subject is still in a stage of vagueness and immaturity. Van Nuysen committed a murder of exceptional atrocity, and afterwards killed himself. Now, bodies of suicides are known to be peculiarly susceptible to spiritual influences, even to the point of arrested corruption. Add to this our knowledge that the highest aim of an evil spirit is to gain possession of a material body. If I carried out my theory to its logical conclusion, I should say that Van Nuysen's body is hidden somewhere on these premises—that this body is intermittently animated by some spirit, which at certain periods is forced to re-enact the gruesome tragedy of the Van Nuysens. Should any living person chance to occupy the position of the first victim, so much the worse for him!'

For some minutes Houston made no remark on this singular expression of opinion.

'But have you ever met with anything of the sort before?' he said at last.

'I can recall,' replied Flaxman Low thoughtfully, 'quite a number of cases which would seem to bear out this hypothesis. Among them a curious problem of haunting exhaustively examined by Busner in the early part of 1888, at which I was myself lucky enough to assist. Indeed, I may add that the affair which I have recently been engaged upon in Vienna offers some rather similar features. There, however, we had to stop short of excavation, by which alone any specific results might have been attained.'

'Then you are of the opinion,' said Houston, 'that pulling the house to pieces might cast some further light upon this affair?'

'I cannot see any better course,' said Mr Low.

Then Houston closed the discussion by a very definite declaration.

'This house shall come down!'

So 'The Spaniards' was pulled down.

The work of demolition, begun at the earliest possible moment, did not occupy very long, and during its early stages, under the boarding at an angle of the landing was found a skeleton. Several of the phalanges were missing, and other indications also established beyond doubt the fact that the remains were the remains of a leper.

The skeleton is now in the museum of one of our city hospitals. It bears a scientific ticket, and is the only evidence extant of the correctness of Mr Flaxman Low's methods and the possible truth of his extraordinary theories.

A WORM'S TURNING

John Eyton

He was a nameless hill labourer—a natural slave if ever there was one. He was utterly out of keeping with these days of Labour Unions and limited hours and representative government—an anachronism, a survival of the days when men were herded and driven. It was such as he who laboured in old-time quarries, and drove galleys, and piled the pyramids. So he was out of his time, a blot on the landscape, and a mockery at the beneficent government which professed such high care for the untutored masses of India. Yet he was not alone; he toiled with hundreds of his kind—men and women—along the mountain way leading to Bhawali. He was a carrier of woods; Heaven knows how many times a day his task was to carry a great solid block of Sal wood—six feet by one foot six by six inches, or something like it—for a mile and a half up the hot, dusty path.

He was only familiar to me because he was older than the rest. His face was seamed and lined, and his hair grey. He carried his solid block of wood on his back, length ways; a rope passed across his forehead—which was bound with a dirty cloth—and another rope under his arms. He lived stooping forwards. The weight was obviously as much as he could stand; he was just able to put one foot before the other, and the muscles of his calves and thighs always trembled. He looked perpetually on the ground, with eyes that started a little out of his head staring. They had no expression, save of intense strain. They saw nothing, noted nothing. They were the eyes of an animal—or of a slave.

Sweat poured from his face and limbs, for all that he wore only a little wisp of dingy cloth round his waist and loins. It was obviously a tremendous effort to him to move out of the path for a rider to pass. When he did, it was with the stumbling, tottering gait of a blind beast of burden.

When he rested for a few minutes, he still could not escape his plank: he had to stand upright, with the plank resting against the wall of rock at the roadside. His face on these occasions showed utter weariness—the other men talked and laughed; but with him it was as if life had been squeezed out, leaving but a blind automaton. He would rest in silence—then get up and plod wearily on.

He had a little time off for food; otherwise he did a full day's—work that a beast would have done in the plains, and that a rope railway might have done years ago in the hills. He had no encouragement; there was no question of efficiency or dispatch; pay was according to the weight carried on each journey, and the sole standard of ability was weight-carrying capacity. There was no pension for long service; he and his kind carried wood—or heavy cases or pianos, as the case might be—until they dropped. At night he must have slept the sleep of a worn-out beast. If he thought at all, he must have been haunted by the fear—'One day I shall not be able to get up with the wood when they load me. The babu will send me away.' Then release—utter poverty—death. He could hardly have escaped that thought—he was so clearly past the work.

I knew the babu by sight; he was the pay-clerk of the local contractor to the Forest Department. I have reason to believe that he took his toll of the labourers—a small commission for employment; perhaps an anna in the rupee; only six percent. His name was Debi Datt—a tall, weedy specimen, who affected English dress and perched his little cap jauntily on the side of his head. He had a black moustache, shifty brown eyes, thick lips, and no chin. He walked about with the swagger of a cavalryman and the assurance of a millionaire—but you could have blown him over easily enough. I also know that he had run through a number of clerkships in various offices, earning the encomiums of 'incorrigibly lazy', 'insufferably idle', 'utterly untrustworthy', and so on. The Forest contractor had taken him on because he was his nephew, and cheap. The latter word aptly describes him.

I did not see the finale between the babu and the man, but I heard the account of an eyewitness.

It happened on the hottest day of the year in the hills— just before the rains. Debi Datt was dispatching—telling off the men's burdens, weighing them, and noting them in his little book. The labourers moved slowly off in parties of six. The weighing was done at a point where the mountain path broadened to a width of seven or eight yards, thus giving room for a clearing station. Below, as usual, there was a steep khud—a sheer drop of fifty feet.

The turn of the old man came, and he moved forward for his burden to be adjusted. It was a particularly massive piece of timber; an ordinary person would have found it difficult to raise one end of it off the ground. The old man murmured something, to which the babu replied roughly. The timber was duly adjusted; the order was given—'Chalo!' The old man strained to raise himself, but failed. He looked round at the babu with a world of pathos in his eyes, as if to say 'You have me beaten at last.' The look was that of an animal—asking for nothing, hoping for nothing—accepting fate. But he did not give up. Again and again he strained, groaning at the weight. At last he really did almost stand up—his joints cracking—then collapsed again.

It was then that the babu kicked him—once, twice, in the ribs with his pointed shoe. There was a grunt of pain, like a sob, and then the unique thing happened. Without an alteration of expression, but with a gigantic heave of the whole body, the old man was on his feet. He stood for the slightest instant, feeling his balance, and then swung sharply round. The whole weight of the butt of timber struck the babu, sweeping him back, spinning him over the khud.

Then the old man overbalanced and followed him, the timber bumping against the rocks. There were two dull thuds a long way below… No worm had ever turned more effectively.

THE DECOY

Algernon Blackwood

It belonged to the category of unlovely houses about which an ugly superstition clings, one reason being, perhaps, its inability to inspire interest in itself without assistance. It seemed too ordinary to possess individuality, much less to exert an influence. Solid and ungainly, its huge bulk dwarfing the park timber, its best claim to notice was a negative one—it was unpretentious.

From the little hill its expressionless windows stared across the Kentish Weald, indifferent to weather, dreary in winter, bleak in spring, unblessed in summer. Some colossal hand had tossed it down, then let it starve to death, a country mansion that might well strain the adjectives of advertisers and find inheritors with difficulty. Its soul had fled, said some; it had committed suicide, thought others; and it was an inheritor, before he killed himself in the library, who thought this latter, yielding, apparently, to a hereditary taint in the family. For two other inheritors followed suit, with an interval of twenty years between them, and there was no clear reason to explain the three disasters. Only the first owner, indeed, lived permanently in the house, the others using it in the summer months and then deserting it with relief. Hence, when John Burley, present inheritor, assumed possession, he entered a house about which clung an ugly superstition, based, nevertheless, upon a series of undeniably ugly facts.

This century deals harshly with superstitious folk, deeming them fools or charlatans; but John Burley, robust, contemptuous of half lights, did not deal harshly with them, because he did not deal with them at all. He was hardly aware of their existence. He ignored them as he ignored, say, the Esquimaux, poets, and other human aspects that did not touch his scheme of life. A successful businessman, he concentrated on what was real; he dealt with business people. His philanthropy, on a big scale, was also real; yet, though he would have denied it vehemently, he had his superstition as well. No man exists without some taint of superstition in his blood; the racial heritage is too rich to be escaped entirely. Burley's took this form—that unless he gave his tithe to the poor he would not prosper. This ugly mansion, he decided, would make an ideal Convalescent Home.

'Only cowards or lunatics kill themselves,' he declared flatly, when his use of the house was criticized. 'I'm neither one nor t'other.' He let out his gusty, boisterous laugh. In his invigorating atmosphere such weakness seemed contemptible, just as superstition in his presence seemed the feeblest ignorance. Even its picturesqueness faded. 'I can't conceive,' he boomed, 'can't even imagine to myself,' he added emphatically, 'the state of mind in which a man can *think* of suicide, much less do it.' He threw his chest out with a challenging air. 'I tell you, Nancy, it's either cowardice or mania. And I've no use for either.'

Yet he was easy-going and good-humoured in his denunciation. He admitted his limitations with a hearty laugh which his wife called noisy. Thus he made allowances for the fairy fears of sailorfolk, and had even been known to mention haunted ships his companies owned. But he did so in the terms of tonnage and £ s.d. His scope was big; details were made for clerks.

His consent to pass a night in the mansion was the consent of a practical businessman and philanthropist who dealt condescendingly with foolish human nature. It was based on the commonsense of tonnage and £ s.d. The local newspapers had revived the silly story of the suicides, calling attention to the effect of the superstition upon the fortunes of the house, and so, possibly, upon the fortunes of its present owner. But the mansion, otherwise a white elephant, was precisely ideal for his purpose, and so trivial a matter as spending a night in it should not stand in the way. 'We must take people as we find them, Nancy.'

His young wife had her motive, of course, in making the proposal, and, if she was amused by what she called 'spook-hunting', he saw no reason to refuse her the indulgence. He loved her, and took her as he found her—late in life. To allay the superstitions of prospective staff and patients and supporters, all, in fact, whose goodwill was necessary to success, he faced this boredom of a night in the building before its opening was announced. 'You see, John, if you, the owner, do this, it will nip damaging talk in the bud. If anything went wrong later it would only be put down to this suicide idea, this haunting influence. The home will have a bad name from the start. There'll be endless trouble. It will be a failure.'

'You think my spending a night there will stop the nonsense?' he enquired.

'According to the old legend it breaks the spell,' she replied. 'That's the condition, anyhow.'

'But somebody's sure to die there sooner or later,' he

objected.

'We can't prevent that. We can prevent people whispering that they died unnaturally.' She explained the working of the public mind.

'I see,' he replied, his lip curling, yet quick to gauge the truth of what she told him about collective instinct.

'Unless *you* take poison in the hall,' she added laughingly, 'or elect to hang yourself with your braces from the hat peg.'

'I'll do it,' he agreed, after a moment's thought. 'I'll sit up with you. It will be like a honeymoon over again, you and I on the spree—eh?' He was even interested now; the boyish side of him was touched perhaps; but his enthusiasm was less when she explained that three was a better number than two on such an expedition.

'I've often done it before, John. We were always three.'

'Who?' he asked bluntly. He looked wonderingly at her, but she answered that if anything went wrong a party of three provided a better margin for help. It was sufficiently obvious. He listened and agreed. 'I'll get young Mortimer,' he suggested. 'Will he do?'

She hesitated. 'Well—he's cheery; he'll be interested, too. Yes, he's as good as another.' She seemed indifferent.

'And he'll make the time pass with his stories,' added her husband.

So Captain Mortimer, late officer on a T.B.D., a 'cheery lad', afraid of nothing, cousin of Mrs Burley, and now filling a good post in the company's London offices, was engaged as third hand in the expedition. But Captain Mortimer was young and ardent, and Mrs Burley was young and pretty and ill-mated, and John Burley was a neglectful and self-satisfied husband.

Fate laid the trap with cunning, and John Burley, blind-eyed, careless of detail, floundered into it. He also floundered out again, though in a fashion none could have expected of him.

The night agreed upon eventually was as near to the shortest in the year as John Burley could contrive—18 June—when the sun set at 8.18 and rose about a quarter to four. There would be barely three hours of true darkness. 'You're the expert,' he admitted, as she explained that only sitting through the actual darkness was required, not necessarily from sunset to sunrise. 'We'll do the thing properly. Mortimer's not very keen, he had a dance or something,' he added, noticing the look of annoyance that flashed swiftly in her eyes, 'but he got out of it. He's coming.' The pouting expression of the spoilt woman amused him. 'Oh, no, he didn't need much persuading really,' he assured her. 'Some girl or other, of course. He's young, remember.' To which no comment was forthcoming, though the implied comparison made her flush.

They motored from South Audley Street after an early tea, in due course passing Sevenoaks and entering the Kentish Weald; and, in order that the necessary advertisement be given, the chauffeur, warned strictly to keep their purpose quiet, was to put up at the country inn and fetch them an hour after sunrise; they would breakfast in London. 'He'll tell everybody,' said his practical and cynical master; 'the local newspaper will have it all next day. A few hours' discomfort is worthwhile if it ends the nonsense. We'll read and smoke, and Mortimer shall tell us yarns about the sea.' He went with the driver into the house to superintend the arrangement of the room, the lights, the hampers of food, and so forth, leaving the pair upon the lawn.

'Four hours isn't much, but it's something,' whispered Mortimer, alone with her for the first time since they started. 'It's simply ripping of you to have got me in. You look divine tonight. You're the most wonderful woman in the world.' His blue eyes shone with the hungry desire he mistook for love. He looked as if he had blown in from the sea, for his skin was tanned and his light hair bleached a little by the sun. He took her hand, drawing her out of the slanting sunlight towards the rhododendrons.

'I didn't, you silly boy. It was John who suggested your coming.' She released her hand with an affected effort. 'Besides, you overdid it—pretending you had a dance.'

'You could have objected,' he said eagerly, 'and didn't. Oh, you're too lovely, you're delicious!' He kissed her suddenly with passion. There was a tiny struggle, in which she yielded too easily, he thought.

'Harry, you're an idiot!' she cried breathlessly, when he let her go. 'I really don't know how you dare! And John's your friend. Besides, you know'—she glanced round quickly— 'it isn't safe here.' Her eyes shone happily, her cheeks were flaming. She looked what she was—a pretty, young, lustful animal, false to ideals, true to selfish passion only. 'Luckily,' she added, 'he trusts me too fully to think anything.'

The young man, worship in his eyes, laughed gaily. 'There's no harm in a kiss,' he said. 'You're a child to him, he never thinks of you as a woman. Anyhow, his head's full of ships and kings and scaling-wax,' he comforted her, while respecting her sudden instinct which warned him not to touch her again, 'and he never sees anything. Why, even at ten yards—'

From twenty yards away a big voice interrupted him, as John Burley came round a corner of the house and across the lawn towards them. The chauffeur, he announced, had left the hampers in the room on the first floor and gone back to the inn. 'Let's take a walk round,' he added, joining them, 'and see the garden. Five minutes before sunset we'll go in and feed.' He laughed. 'We must do the thing faithfully, you know, mustn't we, Nancy? Dark to dark, remember. Come on, Mortimer'—he took the young man's arm—'a last look round before we go in and hang ourselves from adjoining hooks in the matron's room!' He reached out his free hand towards his wife.

'Oh, hush, John!' she said quickly. 'I don't like—especially now the dusk is coming.' She shivered, as though it were a genuine little shiver, pursing her lips deliciously as she did so; whereupon he drew her forcibly to him, saying he was sorry, and kissed her exactly where she had been kissed two minutes before, while young Mortimer looked on. 'We'll take care of you between us,' he said. Behind a broad back the pair exchanged a swift but meaning glance, for there was that in his tone which enjoined wariness, and perhaps after all he was not so blind as he appeared. They had their code, these two. 'All's Well,' was signalled; 'but another time be more careful!'

There still remained some minutes sunlight before the huge red ball of fire would sink behind the wooded hills, and the trio, talking idly, a flutter of excitement to two hearts certainly, walked among the roses. It was a perfect evening, windless, perfumed, warm. Headless shadows preceded them gigantically across the lawn as they moved, and one side of the great building lay already dark; bats were flitting, moths darted to and fro above the azalea and rhododendron clumps. The talk turned chiefly on the uses of the mansion as a Convalescent Home, its probable running cost, suitable staff, and so forth.

'Come along,' John Burley said presently, breaking off and turning abruptly, 'we must be inside, actually inside, before the sun's gone. We must fulfil the conditions faithfully,' he repeated as though fond of the phrase. He was in earnest over everything in life, big or little, once he set his hand to it.

They entered, this incongruous trio of ghost-hunters, not one of them really intent upon the business in hand, and went slowly upstairs to the great room where the hampers lay. Already in the hall it was dark enough for three electric torches to flash usefully and help their steps as they moved with caution, lighting one corner after another. The air inside was chill and damp. 'Like an unused museum,' said Mortimer. 'I can smell the specimens.' They looked about them, sniffing. 'That's humanity,' declared his host, employer, friend, 'with cement and whitewash to flavour it'; and all three laughed as Mrs Burley said she wished they had picked some roses and brought them in. Her husband was again in front on the broad staircase, Mortimer just behind him, when she called out. 'I don't like being last,' she exclaimed. 'It's so black behind me in the hall. I'll come between you two,' and the sailor took her outstretched hand, squeezing it, as he passed her up. 'There's a figure, remember,' she said hurriedly turning to gain her husband's attention, as when she touched wood at home. 'A figure is seen; that's part of the story. The figure of a man.' She gave a tiny shiver of pleasure, half-imagined alarm as she took his arm.

'I hope we shall see it,' he mentioned prosaically.

'I hope we shan't,' she replied with emphasis. 'It's only seen before—something happens.' Her husband said nothing, while Mortimer remarked facetiously that it would be a pity if they had their trouble for nothing. 'Something can hardly happen to all three of us,' he said lightly, as they entered a large room where the paper-hangers had conveniently left a rough table of bare planks. Mrs Burley, busy with her own thoughts, began to unpack the sandwiches and wine. Her husband strolled over to the window. He seemed restless.

'So this'—his deep voice startled her—'is where one of us'—he looked round him—'is to—'

'John!' She stopped him sharply, with impatience. 'Several times already I've begged you.' Her voice rang rather shrill and querulous in the empty room, a new note in it. She was beginning to feel the atmosphere of the place, perhaps. On the sunny lawn it had not touched her, but now, with the fall of night, she was aware of it, as shadow called to shadow and the kingdom of darkness gathered power. Like a great whispering gallery, the whole house listened.

'Upon my word, Nancy,' he said with contrition, as he came and sat down beside her, 'I quite forgot again. Only I cannot take it seriously. It's utterly unthinkable to me that a man—'

'But why evoke the idea at all?' she insisted in a lowered voice, that snapped despite its faintness. 'Men, after all, don't do such things for nothing.'

'We don't know everything in the universe, do we?' Mortimer put in, trying clumsily to support her. 'All I know just now is that I'm famished and this veal and ham pie is delicious.' He was very busy with his knife and fork. His foot rested lightly on her own beneath the table; he could not keep his eyes off her face; he was continually passing new edibles to her.

'No,' agreed John Burley, 'not everything. You're right there.'

She kicked the younger man gently, flashing a warning with her eyes as well, while her husband, emptying his glass, his head thrown back, looked straight at them over the rim, apparently seeing nothing. They smoked their cigarettes round the table, Burley lighting a big cigar. 'Tell us about the figure, Nancy?' he inquired. 'At least there's no harm in that. It's new to me. I hadn't heard about a figure.' And she did so willingly, turning her chair sideways from the dangerous, reckless feet.

Mortimer could now no longer touch her. 'I know very little,' she confessed; 'only what the paper said. It's a man and he changes.'

'How changes?' asked her husband. 'Clothes, you mean, or what?'

Mrs Burley laughed, as though she was glad to laugh. Then she answered: 'According to the story he shows himself each time to the man—'

'The man who—?'

'Yes, yes, of course. He appears to the man who dies—as himself.'

'H'm,' grunted her husband, naturally puzzled. He stared at her.

'Each time the chap saw his own double'—Mortimer came this time usefully to the rescue—'before he did it.'

Considerable explanation followed, involving much psychic jargon from Mrs Burley, which fascinated and impressed the sailor, who thought her as wonderful as she was lovely, showing it in his eyes for all to see John Burley's attention wandered. He moved over to the window, leaving them to finish the discussion between them; he took no part in it, made no comment even, merely listening idly and watching them with an air of absent-mindedness through the cloud of cigar smoke round his head. He moved from window to window, ensconcing himself in turn in each deep embrasure, examining the fastenings, measuring the thickness of the stonework with his handkerchief. He seemed restless, bored, obviously out of place in this ridiculous expedition. On his big massive face lay a quiet, resigned expression his wife had never seen before. She noticed it now as the discussion ended, and the pair tidied away the debris of dinner, lit the spirit lamp for coffee and laid out a supper which would be very welcome with the dawn. A draught passed through the room, making the papers flutter on the table. Mortimer turned down the smoking lamps with care.

'Wind's getting up a bit—from the south,' observed Burley from his niche, closing one-half of the casement window as he said it. To do this, he turned his back a moment, fumbling for several seconds with the latch, while Mortimer, noting it, seized his sudden opportunity with the foolish abandon of his age and temperament. Neither he nor his victim perceived that, against the outside darkness, the interior of the room was plainly reflected in the window-pane. One reckless, the other terrified, they snatched the fearful joy, which might, after all, have been lengthened by another full half-minute, for the head they feared, followed by the shoulders, pushed through the side of the casement still open, and remained outside, taking in the night.

'A grand air,' said his deep voice, as the head drew in again. 'I'd like to be at sea a night like this.' He left the casement open and came across the room towards them. 'Now,' he said cheerfully, arranging a seat for himself, 'let's get comfortable for the night. Mortimer, we expect stories from you without ceasing, until dawn or the ghost arrives. Horrible stories of chains and headless men, remember. Make it a night we shan't forget in a hurry.' He produced his gust of laughter.

They arranged their chairs, with other chairs to put their feet on, and Mortimer contrived a footstool by means of a hamper for the smallest feet; the air grew thick with tobacco smoke; eyes flashed and answered, watched perhaps as well; ears listened and perhaps grew wise; occasionally, as a window shook, they started and looked around; there were sounds about the house from time to time, when the entering wind, using broken or open windows, set loose objects rattling.

But Mrs Burley vetoed horrible stories with decision. A big, empty mansion, lonely in the country, and even with the comfort of John Burley and a lover in it, has its atmosphere. Furnished rooms are far less ghostly. This atmosphere now came creeping everywhere, through spacious halls and sighing corridors, silent, invisible, but all-pervading, John Burley alone impervious to it, unaware of its soft attack upon the nerves. It entered possibly with the summer night wind, but possibly it was always there and Mrs Burley looked often at her husband, sitting near her at an angle; the light fell on his fine strong face; she felt that, though apparently so calm and quiet, he was really very restless; something about him was a little different; she could not define it; his mouth seemed set as with an effort; he looked, she thought curiously to herself, patient and very dignified; he was rather a dear after all. Why did she think the face inscrutable? Her thoughts wandered vaguely, unease, discomfort among them somewhere, while the heated blood—she had taken her share of wine—seethed in her.

Burley turned to the sailor for more stories. 'Sea and wind in them,' he asked. 'No horrors, remember!' And Mortimer told a tale about the shortage of rooms at a Welsh seaside place where spare rooms fetched fabulous prices, and one man alone refused to let—a retired captain of South Seas trader, very poor, a bit crazy apparently. He had two furnished rooms in his house worth twenty guineas a week. The rooms faced south; he kept them full of flowers; but he would not let. An explanation of his unworldly obstinacy was not forthcoming until Mortimer—they fished together—gained his confidence. 'The South Wind lives in them,' the old fellow told him. 'I keep them free for her.'

'For *her*?'

'It was on the South Wind my love came to me,' said the other softly; 'and it was on the South Wind that she felt—'

It was an odd tale to tell in such company, but he told it well.

'Beautiful,' thought Mrs Burley. Aloud she said a quiet, 'Thank you. By 'left' I suppose he meant she died or ran away?'

John Burley looked up with a certain surprise. 'We ask for a story,' he said, 'and you give us a poem.' He laughed. 'You're in love, Mortimer,' he informed him, 'and with my wife, probably.'

'Of course I am, sir,' replied the young man gallantly. 'A sailor's heart, you know,' while the face of the woman turned pink, then white. She knew her husband more intimately than Mortimer did, and there was something in his tone, his eyes, his words, she did not like. Harry was an idiot to choose such a tale. An irritated annoyance stirred in her, close upon dislike. 'Anyhow, it's better than horrors,' she said hurriedly.

'Well,' put in her husband, letting forth a minor gust of laughter, 'it's possible, at any rate. Though one's as crazy as the other.' His meaning, was not wholly clear. 'If a man really loved,' he added in his blunt fashion, 'and was tricked by her, I could almost conceive his—'

'Oh, don't preach, John, for Heaven's sake. You're so dull in the pulpit.' But the interruption only served to emphasize the sentence which, otherwise, might have been passed over.

'Could conceive his finding life so worthless,' persisted the other, 'that—' He hesitated. 'But there, now, I promised I wouldn't,' he went on, laughing good-humouredly. Then, suddenly, as though in spite of himself, driven it seemed: 'Still, under such conditions he might show his contempt for human nature and for life by—'

It was a tiny stifled scream that stopped him this time.

'John, I hate, I loathe you, when you talk like that. And

you've broken your word again.' She was more than petulant; a nervous anger sounded in her voice. It was the way he had said it, looking from them towards the window, that made her quiver. She felt him suddenly as a man; she felt afraid of him.

Her husband made no reply; he rose and looked at his watch leaning sideways towards the lamp, so that the expression of his face was shaded. 'Two o'clock,' he remarked. 'I think I'll take a turn through the house. I may find a workman asleep or something. Anyhow the light will soon come now.' He laughed; the expression of his face, his tone of voice, relieved her momentarily. He went out. They heard his heavy tread echoing down the carpetless long corridor.

Mortimer began at once. 'Did he mean anything?' he asked breathlessly. 'He doesn't love you the least little bit, anyhow. He never did. I do. You're wasted on him. You belong to me.' The words poured out. He covered her face with kisses. 'Oh, I didn't mean *that*,' he caught between the kisses.

The sailor released her, staring. 'What then?' he whispered. 'Do you think he saw us on the lawn?' he paused a moment, as she made no reply. The steps were audible in the distance still. 'I know!' he exclaimed suddenly. 'It's the blessed house he feels. That's what it is. He doesn't like it.'

A wind sighed through the room, making the papers flutter; something rattled; and Mrs Burley started. A loose end of rope swinging from the paperhanger's ladder caught her eye. She shivered slightly.

'He's different,' she replied in a low voice, nestling very close again, 'and so restless. Didn't you notice what he said just now—that under certain conditions he could understand a man'—she hesitated—'doing it,' she concluded, a sudden drop in her voice. 'Harry,' she looked full into his eyes, 'that's not like him. He didn't say that for nothing.'

'Nonsense! He's bored to tears, that's all. And the house is getting on your nerves, too.' He kissed her tenderly. Then, as she responded, he drew her nearer still and held her passionately, mumbling incoherent words, among which 'nothing to be afraid of' was distinguishable. Meanwhile, the steps were coming nearer. She pushed him away. 'You must behave yourself. I insist. You shall, Harry.' Then buried herself in his arms, her face hidden against his neck—only to disentangle herself the next instant and stand clear of him. 'I hate you, Harry,' she exclaimed sharply, a look of angry annoyance flashing across her face. 'And I *hate* myself. Why do you treat me—?' She broke off as the steps came closer, patted her hair straight, and stalked over to the open window.

'I believe after all you're only playing with me,' he said viciously. He stared in surprised disappointment, watching her. 'It's him you really love,' he added jealously. He looked and spoke like a petulant spoilt boy.

She did not turn her head. 'He's always been fair to me, kind and generous. He never blames me for anything. Give me a cigarette, and don't play the stage hero. My nerves are on edge, to tell you the truth.' Her voice jarred harshly, and as he lit her cigarette he noticed that her lips were trembling; his own hand trembled too. He was still holding the match, standing beside her at the window sill, when the steps crossed the threshold and John Burley came into the room. He went straight up to the table and turned the lamp down. 'It was smoking,' he remarked. 'Didn't you see?'

'I'm sorry, sir.' And Mortimer sprang forward too late to help him. 'It was the draught as you pushed the door open.' The big man said, 'Ah!' and drew a chair over, facing them. 'It's just the very house,' he told them. 'I've been through every room on this floor. It will make a splendid home, with very little alteration, too.' He turned round in his creaking wicker chair and looked up at his wife, who sat swinging her legs and smoking in the window embrasure. 'Lives will be saved inside these old walls. It's a good investment,' he went on, talking rather to himself it seemed. 'People will die here, too.'

'Hark!' Mrs Burley interrupted him. 'That noise—What is it?' A faint thudding sound in the corridor or in the adjoining room was audible, making all three look round quickly, listening for a repetition, which did not come. The papers fluttered on the table, the lamps smoked an instant.

'Wind,' observed Burley calmly, 'our little friend, the South Wind. Something blown over again, that's all.' But, curiously, the three of them stood up. 'I'll go and see,' he continued. 'Doors and windows are all open to let the paint dry.' Yet he did not move; he stood there watching a white moth that dashed round and round the lamp, flopping heavily now and again upon the bare deal table.

'Let me go, sir,' put in Mortimer eagerly. He was glad of the chance; for the first time he, too, felt uncomfortable. But there was another, who, apparently, suffered a discomfort greater than his own and was accordingly even more glad to get away. 'I'll go,' Mrs Burley announced, with decision. 'I'd like to. I haven't been out of this room since we came. I'm not an atom afraid.'

It was strange that for a moment she did not make a move either; it seemed as if she waited for something. For perhaps fifteen seconds no one stirred or spoke. She knew by the look in her lover's eyes that he had now become aware of the slight, indefinite change in her husband's manner, and was alarmed by it. The fear in him woke her contempt; she suddenly despised the youth, and was conscious of a new, strange yearning towards her husband; against her worked nameless pressure, troubling her being. There was an alteration in the room, she thought; something had come in. The trio stood listening to the gentle wind outside, waiting for the sound to be repeated; two careless, passionate young lovers and a man stood waiting, listening, watching in that room; yet it seemed there were five persons altogether and not three, for two guilty consciences stood apart and separate from their owners. John Burley broke the silence.

'Yes, you go, Nancy. Nothing to be afraid of—there. It's only the wind.' He spoke as though he meant it.

Mortimer bit his lips. 'I'll come with you,' he said instantly. He was confused. 'Let's all three go. I don't think we ought to be separated.' But Mrs Burley was already at the door. 'I insist,' she said, with a forced laugh. 'I'll call if I'm frightened,' while her husband, saying nothing, watched her from the table.

'Take this,' said the sailor, flashing his electric torch as he went over to her. 'Two are better than one.' He saw her figure exquisitely silhouetted against the black corridor beyond; it was clear she wanted to go; any nervousness in her was mastered by a stronger emotion still; she was glad to be out of their presence for a bit. He had hoped to snatch a word of explanation in the corridor, but her manner stopped him. Something else stopped him, too.

'First door on the left,' he called out, his voice echoing down the empty length. 'That's the room where the noise came from. Shout if you want us.'

He watched her moving away, the light held steadily in front of her, but she made no answer, and he turned back to see John Burley lighting his cigar at the lamp chimney, his face thrust forward as he did so. He stood a second, watching him, as the lips sucked hard at the cigar to make it draw; the strength of the features was emphasized to sternness. He had meant to stand by the door and listen for the least sound from the adjoining room, but now found his whole attention focussed on the face above the lamp. In that minute he realized that Burley had wished—had meant—his wife to go. In that minute he also forgot his love, his shameless, selfish little mistress, his worthless, caddish little self. For John Burley looked up. He straightened slowly, puffing hard and quickly to make sure his cigar was lit, and faced him. Mortimer moved forward into the room, self-conscious, embarrassed, cold.

'Of course, it was only the wind,' he said lightly, his one desire being to fill the interval while they were alone with commonplaces. He did not wish the other to speak. 'Dawn wind, probably.' He glanced at his wrist-watch. 'It's half-past two already and the sun gets up at a quarter to four. It's light by now, I expect. The shortest night is never quite dark.' He rambled on confusedly, for the other's steady, silent stare embarrassed him. A faint sound of Mrs Burley moving in the next room made him stop a moment. He turned instinctively to the door, eager for an excuse to go.

'That's nothing,' said Burley, speaking at last and in a firm quiet voice. 'Only my wife, glad to be alone—my young and pretty wife. She's all right. I know her better than you do. Come in and shut the door.'

Mortimer obeyed. He closed the door and came close to the table, facing the other, who at once continued.

'If I thought,' he said, in that quiet deep voice, 'that you two were serious'—he uttered his words very slowly, with emphasis, with intense severity—'do you know what I should do? I will tell you, Mortimer. I should like one of us two—you or myself—to remain in this house, dead.'

His teeth gripped his cigar tightly; his hands were clenched; he went on through a half-closed mouth. His eyes blazed steadily.

'I trust her so absolutely—understand me?—that my belief in women, in human beings, would go. And with it the desire to live. Understand me?'

Each word to the young careless fool was a blow in the face, yet it was the softest blow, the flash of a big deep heart, that hurt the most. A dozen answers—denial, explanation, confession, taking all guilt upon himself—crowded his mind, only to be dismissed. He stood motionless and silent, staring hard into the other's eyes. No word passed his lips; there was no time in any case. It was in this position that Mrs Burley, entering at that moment, found them. She saw her husband's face; the other man stood with his back to her. She came in with a little nervous laugh. 'A bell-rope swinging in the wind and hitting a sheet of metal before the fireplace,' she informed them. And all three laughed together then, though each laugh had a different sound. 'But I hate this house,' she added. 'I wish we had never come.'

'The moment there's light in the sky,' remarked her husband quietly, 'we can leave. That's the contract; let's see it through. Another half-hour will do it. Sit down, Nancy, and have a bit of something.' He got up and placed a chair for her. 'I think I'll take another look around.' He moved slowly to the door. 'I may go out on to the lawn a bit, and see what the sky is doing.'

It did not take half a minute to say the words, yet to Mortimer it seemed as though the voice would never end. His mind was confused and troubled. He loathed himself, he loathed the woman through whom he had got into this awkward mess.

The situation had suddenly become extremely painful; he had never imagined such a thing; the man he had thought blind had after all seen everything—known it all along, watched them, waited. And the woman, he was now certain, loved her husband; she had fooled him, Mortimer, all along, amusing herself.

'I'll come with you, sir. Do let me,' he said suddenly. Mrs Burley stood pale and uncertain between them. She looked scared. What has happened, she was clearly wondering.

'No, no, Harry'—he called him 'Harry' for the first time— 'I'll be back in five minutes at the most. My wife mustn't be alone either.' And he went out.

The young man waited till the footsteps sounded some distance down the corridor, then turned, but he did not move forward; for the first time he let pass unused what he called 'an opportunity'. His passion had left him; his love, as he once thought it, was gone. He looked at the pretty woman near him, wondering blankly what he had ever seen there to attract him so wildly. He wished to Heaven he was out of it all. He wished he were dead. John Burley's words suddenly appalled him.

One thing he saw plainly—she was frightened. This opened his lips.

'What's the matter?' he asked, and his hushed voice shirked the familiar Christian name. 'Did you see anything?' He nodded his head in the direction of the adjoining room. It was the sound of his own voice addressing her coldly that made him abruptly see himself as he really was, but it was her reply, honestly given, in a faint even voice, that told him she saw her own self too with similar clarity. God, he thought, how revealing a tone, a single word can be!

'I saw—nothing. Only I feel uneasy—dear.' That 'dear' was a call for help.

'Look here,' he cried, so loud that she held up a warning finger, 'I'm—I've been a damned fool, a cad! I'm most frightfully ashamed. I'll do *anything*—anything to get it right.' He felt cold, naked, his worthlessness laid bare; she felt, he knew, the same. Each revolted suddenly from the other. Yet, he knew not quite how or wherefore this great change had thus abruptly come about, especially on her side. He felt that a bigger, deeper emotion than he could understand was working on them, making mere physical relationships seem empty, trivial, cheap and vulgar. His cold increased in the face of this utter ignorance.

'Uneasy?' he repeated, perhaps hardly knowing exactly why he said it. 'Good Lord, but he can take care of himself—'

'Oh, *he* is a man,' she interrupted; 'yes.'

Steps were heard, firm, heavy steps, coming back along the corridor. It seemed to Mortimer that he had listened to this sound of steps all night, and would listen to them till he died. He crossed to the lamp and lit a cigarette, carefully this time, turning the wick down afterwards. Mrs Burley also rose, moving towards the door, away from him. They listened a moment to these firm and heavy steps, the tread of a man, John Burley. A man—and a philanderer— flashed across Mortimer's brain like fire, contrasting the two with fierce contempt for himself. The tread became less audible. There was distance in it. It had turned in somewhere.

'There!' she exclaimed in a hushed tone. 'He's gone in.'

'Nonsense! It passed us. He's going out on to the lawn.'

The pair listened breathlessly for a moment, when the sound of steps came distinctly from the adjoining room, walking across the boards, apparently towards the window.

'There!' she repeated. 'He did go in.'

Silence of perhaps a minute followed, in which they heard

each other's breathing. 'I don't like being alone—in there,' Mrs Burley said in a thin faltering voice, and moved as though to go out. Her hand was already on the knob of the door, when Mortimer stopped her with a violent gesture.

'Don't! For God's sake, don't!' he cried, before she could turn it. He darted forward. As he laid a hand upon her arm, a thud was audible through the wall. It was a heavy sound, and this time there was no wind to cause it.

'It's only that loose swinging thing,' he whispered thickly, a dreadful confusion blotting out clear thought and speech.

'There was no loose swaying thing at all,' she said in a failing voice, then reeled and swayed against him. 'I invented that. There was nothing.' As he caught her staring helplessly, it seemed to him that a face with lifted lids rushed up at him. He saw two terrified eyes in a patch of ghastly white. Her whisper followed, as she sank into his arms. 'It's John, he's—'

At which instant, with terror at its climax, the sound of steps suddenly became audible once more—the firm and heavy tread of John Burley coming out again into the corridor. Such was their amazement and relief that they neither moved nor spoke. The steps drew nearer. The pair seemed petrified; Mortimer did not remove his arms, nor did Mrs Burley attempt to release herself. They stared at the door and waited. It was pushed wider the next second, and John Burley stood beside them. He was so close he almost touched them—there in each other's arms.

'Jack, dear!' cried his wife, with a searching tenderness that made her voice seem strange.

He gazed a second at each in turn. 'I'm going out on to the lawn for a moment,' he said quietly. There was no expression on his face; he did not smile, he did not frown; he showed no feeling, no emotion—just looked into their eyes, and then withdrew round the edge of the door before either could utter a word in answer. The door swung to behind him.

He was gone. 'He's going to the lawn. He said so.' It was Mortimer speaking, but his voice shook and stammered. Mrs Burley had released herself. She stood now by the table, silent, gazing with fixed eyes at nothing, her lips parted, her expression vacant. Again, she was aware of an alteration in the room: something had gone out... He watched her a second, uncertain what to say or do. It was the face of a drowned person, occurred to him. Something intangible, yet almost visible stood between them in that narrow space. Something had ended, there before his eyes, definitely ended. The barrier between them rose higher, denser. Through this barrier her words came to him with an odd whispering remoteness.

'Harry. You saw? You noticed?'

'What d'you mean?' he said gruffly. He tried to feel angry, contemptuous, but his breath caught absurdly.

'Harry—he was different. The eyes, the hair, the'—her face grew like death—'the twist in his face—'

'What on earth are you saying? Pull yourself together.' He saw that she was trembling down the whole length of her body, as she leaned against the table for support. His own legs shook. He stared hard at her.

'Altered, Harry altered.' Her horrified whisper came at him like a knife. For it was true. He, too, had noticed something about the husband's appearance that was not quite normal. Yet, even while they talked, they heard him going down the carpetless stairs; the sounds ceased as he crossed the hall; then came the noise of the front door banging, the reverberation even shaking the room a little where they stood.

Mortimer went over to her side. He walked unevenly.

'My dear! For God's sake—this is sheer nonsense. Don't let yourself go like this. I'll put it straight with him—it's all my fault.' He saw by her face that she did not understand his words; he was saying the wrong thing altogether; her mind was utterly elsewhere. 'He's all right,' he went on hurriedly. 'He's not on the lawn now.'

He broke off at the sight of her. The horror that fastened on her brain plastered her face with deathly whiteness.

'That was not John at all,' she cried, a wail of misery and terror in her voice. She rushed to the window and he followed. To his immense relief a figure moving below was plainly visible. It was John Burley. They saw him in the faint grey of the dawn, as he crossed the lawn, going away from the house. He disappeared.

'There you are! See?' whispered Mortimer reassuringly. 'He'll be back in—' when a sound in the adjoining room, heavier, louder than before, cut appallingly across his words, and Mrs Burley, with that wailing scream, fell back into his arms. He caught her only just in time, for he stiffened into ice, daft with the uncomprehended terror of it all, and helpless as a child.

'Darling, my darling—oh, God!' He bent, kissing her face wildly. He was utterly distraught.

'Harry! John—oh, oh!' she wailed in her anguish. 'It took on his likeness. It deceived us to give him time. He's done it.'

She sat up suddenly. 'Go,' she said, pointing to the room beyond, then sank fainting, a dead weight in his arms.

He carried her unconscious body to a chair, then entering the adjoining room he flashed his torch upon the body of her husband hanging from a bracket in the wall. He cut it down five minutes too late.

THE PHANTOM 'RICKSHAW

Rudyard Kipling

May no ill dreams disturb my rest,
Nor Powers of Darkness me molest.

—Evening Hymn

One of the few advantages that India has over England is a great knowability. After five years' service a man is directly or indirectly acquainted with the two or three hundred civilians in his province, all the messes of ten or twelve regiments and batteries, and some fifteen hundred other people of the non-official caste. In ten years his knowledge should be doubled, and at the end of twenty he knows, or knows something about, every Englishman in the Empire, and may travel anywhere and everywhere without paying hotel bills.

Globetrotters who expect entertainment as a right have, even within my memory, blunted this open-heartedness, but nonetheless today, if you belong to the Inner Circle and are neither a Bear nor a Black Sheep, all houses are open to you, and our small world is very, very kind and helpful.

Rickett of Kamartha stayed with Polder of Kumaon some

fifteen years ago. He meant to stay two nights, but was knocked down by rheumatic fever, and for six weeks disorganized Polder's establishment, stopped Polder's work, and nearly died in Polder's bedroom. Polder behaves as though he had been placed under eternal obligation by Rickett, and yearly sends the little Ricketts a box of presents and toys. It is the same everywhere. The men who do not take the trouble to conceal from you their opinion that you are an incompetent ass, and the women who blacken your character and misunderstand your wife's amusements, will work themselves to the bone on your behalf if you fall sick or into serious trouble.

Heatherlegh, the doctor, kept, in addition to his regular practice, a hospital on his private account—an arrangement of loose boxes for incurables, his friend called it—but it was really a sort of fitting-up shed for craft that had been damaged by the stress of weather. The weather in India is often sultry, and since the tale of bricks is always a fixed quantity, and the only liberty allowed is permission to work overtime and get no thanks, men occasionally break down and become as mixed as the metaphors in this sentence.

Heatherlegh is the dearest doctor that ever was, and his invariable prescription to all his patients is, 'Lie low, go slow, and keep cool.' He says that more men are killed by overwork than the importance of this world justifies. He maintains that overwork slew Pansay, who died under his hands about three years ago. He has, of course, the right to speak authoritatively, and he laughs at my theory that there was a crack in Pansay's head and a little bit of the Dark World came through and pressed him to death. 'Pansay went off the handle,' says Heatherlegh, 'after the stimulus of long leave at Home. He may or he may not have behaved like a blackguard to Mrs Keith-Wessington. My notion is that the work of the Katabundi Settlement ran him off his legs, and that he took to brooding and making much of an ordinary E & O flirtation. He certainly was engaged to Miss Mannering, and she certainly broke off the engagement. Then he took a feverish chill and all that nonsense about ghosts developed. Overwork started his illness, kept it alight, and killed him, poor devil. Write him off to the system that uses one man to do the work of two and a half men.'

I do not believe this. I use to sit up with Pansay sometimes when Heatherlegh was called out to patients and I happened to be within claim. The man would make me most unhappy by describing in a low, even voice, the procession that was always passing at the bottom of the bed. He had a sick man's command of language. When he recovered I suggested that he should write out the whole affair from beginning to end, knowing that this might assist him to ease his mind.

He was in a high fever while he was writing, and the blood-and-thunder magazine diction he adopted did not calm him. Two months afterwards he was reported fit for duty, but, in spite of the fact that he was urgently needed to help an undermanned commission stagger through a deficit, he preferred to die; vowing at the last that he was hag-ridden. I got his manuscript before he died, and this is his version of the affair, dated 1885, exactly as he wrote it:

My doctor tells me that I need rest and change of air. It is not improbable that I shall get both ere long-rest that neither the red-coated messenger nor the midday gun can break, and change of air far beyond that which any homeward-bound steamer can give me. In the meantime I am resolved to stay where I am; and, in flat defiance of my doctor's orders, to take all the world into my confidence. You shall learn for yourselves the precise nature of my malady, and shall, too, judge for yourselves whether any man born of woman on this weary earth was ever so tormented as I.

Speaking now as a condemned criminal might speak ere the drop-bolts are drawn, my story, wild and hideously improbable as it may appear, demands at least attention. That it will ever receive credence I utterly disbelieve. Two months ago I should have scouted as mad or drunk the man who had dared tell me the like. Two months ago I was the happiest man in India. Today, from Peshawar to the sea there is no one more wretched. My doctor and I are the only two who know this. His explanation is, that my brain, digestion and eyesight are all slightly affected; giving rise to my frequent and persistent 'delusions'. Delusions, indeed I call him a fool; but he attends me still with the same unwearied smile, the same bland professional manner, the same neatly-trimmed red whiskers, till I begin to suspect that I am an ungrateful, evil-tempered invalid. But you shall judge for yourselves.

Three years ago it was my fortune—my great misfortune—to sail from Gravesend to Bombay, on return from a long leave, with one Agnes Keith-Wessington, wife of an officer on the Bombay side. It does not in the least concern you to know what manner of woman she was. Be content with the knowledge that, ere the voyage had ended, both she and I were desperately and unreasoningly in love with one another. Heaven knows that I can make the admission now without one particle of vanity. In matters of this sort there is always one who gives and another who accepts. From the first day of our ill-omened attachment, I was conscious that Agnes's passion was stronger, more dominant, and—if I may use the expression—a purer sentiment than mine. Whether she recognized the fact then,

I do not know. Afterwards it was bitterly plain to both of us.

Arrived at Bombay in the spring of the year, we went our respective ways, to meet no more for the next three or four months, when my leave and her love took us both to Simla. There we spent the season together; and there my fire *of* straw burnt itself out to a pitiful end with the closing year. I attempt no excuse. I make no apology. Mrs Wessington had given up much for my sake, and was prepared to give up all. From my own lips, in August 1882, she learnt that I was sick of her presence, tired of her company, and weary of the sound of her voice. Ninety-nine women out of a hundred would have wearied of me as I wearied of them; seventy-five of that number would have promptly avenged themselves by active and obtrusive flirtation with other men. Mrs Wessington was the hundredth. On her neither my openly-expressed aversion nor the cutting brutalities with which I garnished our interviews had the least effect.

'Jack, darling!' was her one eternal cuckoo cry. 'I'm sure it's all a mistake—a hideous mistake; and we'll be good friends again some day. *Please* forgive me, Jack, dear.'

I was the offender, and I knew it. That knowledge transformed my pity into passive endurance, and, eventually, into blind hate—the same instinct, I suppose, which prompts a man to savagely stamp on the spider he has but half-killed. And with this hate in my bosom the season of 1882 came to an end.

Next year we met again at Simla—she with her monotonous face and timid attempts at reconciliation, and I with loathing of her in every fibre of my frame. Several times I could not avoid meeting her alone; and on each occasion her words were identically the same. Still the unreasoning wail that it was all a 'mistake'; and still the hope of eventually 'making friends'. I might have seen, had I cared to look, that that hope only was keeping her alive. She grew more wan and thin month by month. You will agree with me, at least, that such conduct would have driven anyone to despair. It was uncalled for; childish; unwomanly. I maintain that she was much to blame. And again, sometimes, in the black, fever-stricken night watches, I have begun to think that I might have been a little kinder to her. But that really *is* a 'delusion'. I could not have continued pretending to love her when I didn't; could I? It would have been unfair to us both.

Last year we met again—on the same terms as before. The same weary appeals, and the same curt answers from my lips. At least I would make her see how wholly wrong and hopeless were her attempts at resuming the old relationship. As the season wore on, we fell apart—that is to say, she found it difficult to meet me, for I had other and more absorbing interests to attend to. When I think it over quietly in my sickroom, the season of 1884 seems a confused nightmare wherein light and shade were fantastically intermingled—my courtship of little Kitty Mannering; my hopes, doubts, and fears; our long rides together; my trembling avowal of attachment; her reply; and now and again a vision of a white face flitting by in the 'rickshaw with the black and white liveries I once watched for so earnestly; the wave of Mrs Wessington's gloved hand; and, when she met me alone, which was but seldom, the irksome monotony of her appeal. I loved Kitty Mannering; honestly, heartily loved her, and with my love for her grew my hatred for Agnes. In August, Kitty and I were engaged. The next day I met those accursed 'magpie' jhampanies at the back of Jakko, and, moved by some passing sentiment of pity, stopped to tell Mrs Wessington everything. She knew it already.

'So I hear you're engaged, Jack dear.' Then, without a

moment's pause: 'I'm sure it's all a mistake—a hideous mistake. We shall be as good friends some day, Jack, as we ever were.'

My answer might have made even a man wince. It cut the dying woman before me like the blow of a whip. 'Please forgive me, Jack; I didn't mean to make you angry; but it's true, it's true!'

And Mrs Wessington broke down completely. I turned away and left her to finish her journey in peace, feeling, but only for a moment or two, that I had been an unutterably mean hound. I looked back, and saw that she had turned her 'rickshaw with the idea, I suppose, of overtaking me.

The scene and its surroundings were photographed on my memory. The rain-swept sky (we were at the end of the wet weather), the sodden, dingy pines, the muddy road, and the black powder-riven cliffs formed a gloomy background against which the black and white liveries of the jhampanies, the yellow-panelled 'rickshaw and Mrs Wessington's down-bowed golden head stood out clearly. She was holding her handkerchief in her left hand and was leaning back exhausted against the 'rickshaw cushions. I turned my horse up a bypath near the Sanjowlie Reservoir and literally ran away. Once I fancied I heard a faint call of 'Jack!'. This may have been imagination. I never stopped to verify it. Ten minutes later I came across Kitty on horseback; and, in the delight of a long ride with her, forgot all about the interview.

A week later Mrs Wessington died, and the inexpressible burden of her existence was removed from my life. I went Plainsward perfectly happy. Before three months were over I had forgotten all about her, except that at times the discovery of some of her old letters reminded me unpleasantly of our bygone relationship. By January, I had disinterred what was left of our correspondence from among my scattered belongings and had burnt it. At the beginning of April of this year, 1885, I was at Simla—semi-deserted Simla—once more, and was deep in lover's talks and walks with Kitty. It was decided that we should be married at the end of June. You will understand, therefore, that, loving Kitty as I did, I am not saying too much when I pronounce myself to have been, at that time, the happiest man in India.

Fourteen delightful days passed almost before I noticed their flight. Then, aroused to the sense of what was proper among mortals, circumstanced as we were, I pointed out to Kitty that an engagement ring was the outward and visible sign of her dignity as an engaged girl; and that she must forthwith come to Hamilton's to be measured for one. Up to that moment, I give you my word, we had completely forgotten so trivial a matter. To Hamilton's we accordingly went on 15 April 1885. Remember that—whatever my doctor may say to the contrary—I was then in perfect health, enjoying a well-balanced mind and an *absolutely* tranquil spirit. Kitty and I entered Hamilton's shop together, and there, regardless of the order of affairs, I measured Kitty for the ring in the presence of the amused assistant. The ring was a sapphire with two diamonds. We men rode out down the slope that leads to the Combermere Bridge and Peliti's shop.

While my Waler was cautiously feeling his way over the loose shale, and Kitty was laughing and chattering at my side while all Simla, that is to say as much of it as had then come from the plains, was grouped round the reading-room and Peliti's verandah, I was aware that someone, apparently at a vast distance, was calling me by my Christian name. It struck me that I had heard the voice before, but when and where I could not at once determine. In the short space it took to cover the road between the path from Hamilton's shop and the first plank of the Combermere Bridge I had thought over half a dozen people who might have committed such a solecism, and had eventually decided that it must have been some singing in my ears. Immediately opposite Peliti's shop my eye was arrested by the sight of four jhampanies in 'magpie' livery, pulling a yellow-panelled, cheap, bazaar 'rickshaw. In a moment my mind flew back to the previous season and Mrs Wessington, with a sense of irritation and disgust. Was it not enough that the woman was dead and done with, without her black and white servitors reappearing to spoil the day's happiness? Whoever employed them now, I thought I would call upon, and ask as a personal favour to change her jhampanies' livery. I would hire the men myself, and, if necessary, buy their coats from off their backs. It is impossible to say here what a flood of undesirable memories their presence evoked.

'Kitty,' I cried, 'there are poor Mrs Wessington's jhampanies turned up again! I wonder who has them now?'

Kitty had known Mrs Wessington slightly last season, and had always been interested in the sickly woman.

'What? Where?' she asked. 'I can't see them anywhere.'

Even as she spoke, her horse, swerving from a laden mule, threw himself directly in front of the advancing 'rickshaw. I had scarcely time to utter a word of warning when, to my unutterable horror, horse and rider passed *through* men and carriage as if they had been thin air.

'What's the matter?' cried Kitty; 'what made you call out so foolishly, Jack? If I *am* engaged I don't want all creation to know about it. There was lots of space between the mule and the verandah; and, if you think I can't ride—There!'

Whereupon the wilful Kitty set off, her dainty little head

in the air, at a hand-gallop in the direction of the Bandstand; fully expecting, as she herself afterwards told me, that I should follow her. What was the matter? Nothing indeed. Either that I was mad or drunk, or that Simla was haunted with devils. I reined in my impatient cob, and turned round. The 'rickshaw had turned too, and now stood immediately facing me, near the left railing of the Combermere Bridge.

'Jack! Jack, darling!' (There was no mistake about the words this time: they rang through my brain as if they had been shouted in my ear.) 'It's some hideous mistake, I'm sure. *Please* forgive me, Jack, and lets' be friends again.'

The 'rickshaw-hood had fallen back, and inside, as I hope and pray daily for the death I dread by night, sat Mrs Keith-Wessington, handkerchief in hand, and golden head bowed on her breast.

How long I stared motionless I do not know. Finally, I was aroused by my syce taking the Waler's bridle and asking whether I was ill. From the horrible to the commonplace is but a step. I tumbled off my horse and dashed, half-fainting, into Peliti's for a glass of cherry-brandy. There two or three couples were gathered round the coffee-tables discussing the gossip of the day. Their trivialities were more comforting to me just then than the consolations of religion could have been. I plunged into the midst of the conversation at once; chatted, laughed and jested with a face (when I caught a glimpse of it in a mirror) as white and drawn as that of a corpse. Three or four men noticed my condition; and, evidently setting it down to the results of over-many pegs, charitably endeavoured to draw me apart from the rest of the loungers. But I refused to be led away. I wanted the company of my kind—as a child rushes into the midst of the dinner-party after a fright in the dark. I must have talked for about ten minutes or so, though it seemed an eternity to me, when I heard Kitty's clear voice outside enquiring for me. In another minute she had entered the shop, prepared to upbraid me for failing so signally in my duties. Something in my face stopped her.

'Why, Jack,' she cried, 'what *have* you been doing? What *has* happened? Are you ill?' Thus driven into a direct lie, I said that the sun had been a little too much for me. it was close upon five o'clock of a cloudy April afternoon, and the sun had been hidden all day. I saw my mistake as soon as the words were out of my mouth: attempted to recover it; blundered hopelessly and followed Kitty, in a regal rage, out of doors, amid the smiles of my acquaintances. I made some excuse (I have forgotten what) on the score of my feeling faint; and cantered away to my hotel, leaving Kitty to finish the ride by herself.

In my room I sat down and tried calmly to reason out the matter. Here was I, Theobald Jack Pansay, a well-educated Bengal Civilian in the year of grace, 1885, presumably sane, certainly healthy, driven in terror from my sweetheart's side by the apparition of a woman who had been dead and buried eight months ago. These were facts that I could not blink. Nothing was further from my thought than any memory of Mrs Wessington when Kitty and I left Hamilton's shop. Nothing was more utterly commonplace than the stretch of wall opposite Peliti's. It was broad daylight. The road was full of people; and yet here, look you, in defiance of every law of probability, in direct outrage of Nature's ordinance, there had appeared to me a face from the grave.

Kitty's Arab had gone *through* the 'rickshaw: so that my first hope that some woman marvellously like Mrs Wessington had hired the carriage and the coolies with their old livery was

lost. Again and again I went round this treadmill of thought;
and again and again gave up baffled and in despair. The voice
was as inexplicable as the apparition. I had originally some wild
notion of confiding it all to Kitty; of begging her to marry me
at once; and in her arms defying the ghostly occupant of the
'rickshaw. 'After all,' I argued, 'the presence of the 'rickshaw is
in itself enough to prove the existence of a spectral illusion. One
may see ghosts of men and women, but surely never coolies
and carriages. The whole thing is absurd. Fancy the ghost of
a hillman!'

Next morning I sent a penitent note to Kitty, imploring
her to overlook my strange conduct of the previous afternoon.
My Divinity was still very wroth, and a personal apology
was necessary. I explained, with a fluency born of night-long
pondering over a falsehood, that I had been attacked with a
sudden palpitation of the heart—the result of indigestion. This
eminently practical solution had its effect: and Kitty and I rode
out that afternoon with the shadow of my first lie dividing us.

Nothing would please her save a canter round Jakko.
With my nerves still unstrung from the previous night I feebly
protested against the notion, suggesting Observatory Hill,
Jutogh, the Boileaugunge road—anything rather than the Jakko
round. Kitty was angry and a little hurt; so I yielded from
fear of provoking further misunderstanding, and we set out
together towards Chhota Simla. We walked a greater part of the
way, and, according to our custom, cantered from a mile or so
below the Convent to the stretch of level road by the Sanjowlie
Reservoir. The wretched horses appeared to fly, and my heart
beat quicker and quicker as we neared the crest of the ascent.
My mind had been full of Mrs Wessington all afternoon; and
every inch of the Jakko road bore witness to our old-time walks

and talks. The bowlders were full of it; the pines sang it aloud overhead; the rain-fed torrents giggled and chuckled unseen over the shameful story; and the wind in my ears chanted the iniquity aloud.

As a fitting climax, in the middle of the level men call the Ladies' Mile the horror was awaiting me. No other 'rickshaw was in sight—only the four black and white jhampanies, the yellow-panelled carriage, and the golden head of the woman within—all apparently just as I had left them eight months and one fortnight ago! For an instant I fancied that Kitty *must* see what I saw—we were so marvellously sympathetic in all things. Her next words undeceived me—'Not a soul in sight! Come along, Jack, and I'll race you to the Reservoir buildings!' Her wiry little Arab was off like a bird, my Waler following close behind, and in this order we dashed under the cliffs. Half a minute brought us within fifty yards of the 'rickshaw. I pulled my Waler and fell back a little. The 'rickshaw was directly in the middle of the road; and once more the Arab passed through it, my horse following. 'Jack! Jack dear! *Please* forgive me,' rang with a wail in my ears, and, after an interval: 'It's all a mistake, a hideous mistake!'

I spurred my horse like a man possessed. When I turned my head at the Reservoir works, the black and white liveries were still waiting—patiently waiting—under the grey hillside, and the wind brought me a mocking echo of the words I had just heard. Kitty bantered me a good deal on my silence throughout the remainder of the ride. I had been talking up till then wildly and at random. To save my life I could not speak afterwards, naturally, and from Sanjowlie to the Church wisely held my tongue.

I was to dine with the Mannerings that night, and had barely time to canter home to dress. On the road to Elysium Hill I overheard two men talking together in the dusk—'It's a curious thing,' said one, 'how completely all trace of it disappeared. You know my wife was insanely fond of the woman (never could see anything in her myself), and wanted me to pick up her old 'rickshaw and coolies if they were to be got for love or money. Morbid sort of fancy I call it; but I've got to do what the Memsahib tells me. Would you believe that the man she hired it from tells me that all four of the men—they were brothers—died of cholera on the way to Haridwar, poor devils; and the 'rickshaw has been broken up by the man himself. Told me he never used a dead Memsahib's 'rickshaw. Spoilt his luck. Queer notion, wasn't it? Fancy poor little Mrs Wessington spoiling anyone's luck except her own!' I laughed aloud at this point; and my laugh jarred on me as I uttered it. So there *were* ghosts of 'rickshaws after all, and ghostly employments in the other world! How much did Mrs Wessington give her men? What were their hours? Where did they go?

And for visible answer to my last question I saw the infernal thing blocking my path in the twilight. The dead travel fast, and by short cuts unknown to ordinary coolies. I laughed aloud a second time and checked my laughter suddenly, for I was afraid I was going mad. Mad to a certain extent I must have been, for I recollect that I reined in my horse at the head of the 'rickshaw, and politely wished Mrs Wessington 'Good-evening'. Her answer was one I knew only too well. I listened to the end; and replied that I had heard it all before, but should be delighted if she had anything further to say; some malignant devil stronger than I must have entered into me that evening, for I have a dim recollection of talking the commonplaces of the day for five minutes to the thing in front of me.

'Mad as a hatter, poor devil—or drunk. Max, try and get him to come home.'

Surely *that* was not Mrs Wessington's voice! The two men had overheard me speaking to the empty air, and had returned to look after me. They were very kind and considerate, and from their words evidently gathered that I was extremely drunk. I thanked them confusedly and cantered away to my hotel, there changed, and arrived at the Mannerings' ten minutes late. I pleaded the darkness of the night as an excuse; was rebuked by Kitty for my unlover-like tardiness; and sat down.

The conversation had already become general; and under cover of it, I was addressing some tender small talk to my sweetheart when I was aware that at the further end of the table a short red-whiskered man was describing, with much broidery, his encounter with a mad unknown that evening.

A few sentences convinced me that he was repeating the incident of half an hour ago. In the middle of the story he looked around for applause, as professional story tellers do, caught my eye, and straightway collapsed. There was a moment's awkward silence, and the red-whiskered man muttered something to the effect that he had 'forgotten the rest', thereby sacrificing a reputation as a good storyteller which he had built up for six seasons past. I blessed him from the bottom of my heart, and—went on with my fish.

In the fullness of time that dinner came to an end; and with genuine regret I tore myself away from Kitty—as certain as I was of my own existence that it would be waiting for me outside the door. The red-whiskered man, who had been introduced to me as Dr Heatherlegh of Simla, volunteered to bear me company as far as our roads lay together. I accepted his offer with gratitude.

My instinct had not deceived me. It lay in readiness in the Mall, and, in what seemed devilish mockery of our ways, with a lighted head lamp. The red-whiskered man went to the point at once, in a manner that showed he had been thinking over it all dinner-time.

'I say, Pansay, what the deuce was the matter with you this evening on the Elysium Road?' The suddenness of the question wrenched an answer from me before I was aware.

'That!' said I, pointing to it.

'*That* may be either D.T. or eyes for aught I know. Now you don't liquor. I saw as much at dinner, so it can't be D.T. There's nothing whatever where you're pointing, though you're sweating and trembling with fright, like a scared pony. Therefore, I conclude that it's eyes. And I ought to understand all about them. Come along home with me. I'm on the Blessington lower road.'

To my intense delight the 'rickshaw instead of waiting for us kept about twenty yards ahead—and this, too, whether we walked, trotted, or cantered. In the course of that long night ride I had told my companion almost as much as I have told you here.

'Well, you've spoilt one of the best tales I've ever laid tongue to,' said he, 'but I'll forgive you for the sake of what you've gone through. Now come home and do what I tell you; and when I've cured you, young man, let this be a lesson to you to steer clear of women and indigestible food till the day of your death.'

The 'rickshaw kept steady in front; and my red-whiskered friend seemed to derive great pleasure from my account of its exact whereabouts.

'Eyes, Pansay—all eyes, brain and stomach. And the greatest

of these three is stomach. You've too much conceited brain, too little stomach, and thoroughly unhealthy eyes. Get your stomach straight and the rest follows. And all that's French for a liver pill. I'll take sole medical charge of you from this hour! For you're too interesting a phenomenon to be passed over.'

By this time we were deep in the shadow of the Blessington lower road and the 'rickshaw came to a dead stop under a pine-clad, overhanging shale cliff. Instinctively I halted too, giving my reason, Heatherlegh rapped out an oath.

'Now, if you think I'm going to spend a cold night on the hillside for the sake of a stomach-cum-brain-cum-eye illusion—Lord have mercy! What's that?'

There was a muffled report, a blinding smother of dust just in front of us, a crack, the noise of rent boughs, and about ten yards of the cliff-side—pines, undergrowth, and all—slid down into the road below, completely blocking it up. The uprooted trees swayed and tottered for a moment like drunken giants in the gloom, and then fell prone among their fellows with a thunderous crash. Our two horses stood motionless and sweating with fear. As soon as the rattle of falling earth and stone had subsided, my companion muttered: 'Man, if we'd gone forward we should have been ten feet deep in our graves by now. "There are more things in heaven and earth…" Come home, Pansay, and thank God. I want a peg badly.'

We retraced our way over the Church Ridge, and I arrived at Dr Heatherlegh's house shortly after midnight.

His attempts towards my cure commenced almost immediately, and for a week I never left his sight. Many a time in the course of that week did I bless the good fortune which had thrown me in contact with Simla's best and kindest doctor. Day by day my spirits grew lighter and more equable. Day by day, too,

I became more and more inclined to fall in with Heatherlegh's 'spectral illusion' theory, implicating the eyes, brain, and stomach. I wrote to Kitty, telling her that a slight sprain caused by a fall from my horse kept me indoors for a few days; and that I should be recovered before she had time to regret my absence.

Heatherlegh's treatment was simple to a degree. It consisted of liver pills, cold-water baths, and strong exercise, taken in the dusk or at early dawn—for, as he sagely observed: 'A man with a sprained ankle doesn't walk a dozen miles a day, and your young woman might be wondering if she saw you.'

At the end of the week, after much examination of pupil and pulse, and strict injunctions as to diet and pedestrianism, Heatherlegh dismissed me as brusquely as he had taken charge of me. Here is his parting benediction: 'Man, I certify to your mental cure, and that's as much as to say I've cured most of your bodily ailments. Now, get your traps out of this as soon as you can; and be off to make love to Miss Kitty.'

I was endeavouring to express my thanks for his kindness. He cut me short.

'Don't think I did this because I like you. I gather that you've behaved like a blackguard all through. But, all the same, you're a phenomenon, and as queer a phenomenon as you are a blackguard. No!'—checking me a second time—'not a rupee, please. Go out and see if you can find the eyes-brain-and-stomach business again. I'll give you a lakh for each time you see it.'

Half an hour later I was in the Mannerings' drawing-room with Kitty—drunk with the intoxication of the present happiness and the foreknowledge that I should never more be troubled with its hideous presence. Strong in the sense of my new-found security, I proposed a ride at once; and, by preference, a canter round Jakko.

Never had I felt so well, so overladen with vitality and mere animal spirits, as I did on the afternoon of the 30 April. Kitty was delighted at the change in my appearance, and complimented me on it in her delightfully frank and outspoken manner. We left the Mannerings' house together, laughing and talking, and cantered along the Chhota Simla road as of old.

I was in haste to reach the Sanjowlie Reservoir and there make my assurance doubly sure. The horses did their best, but seemed all too slow to my impatient mind. Kitty was astonished at my boisterousness. 'Why, Jack!' she cried at last, 'you are behaving like a child. What are you doing?'

We were just below the Convent, and from sheer wantonness I was making my Waler plunge and curvet across the road as I tickled it with the loop of my riding-whip.

'Doing?' I answered; 'nothing, dear. That's just it. If you'd been doing nothing for a week except lie up, you'd be as riotous as I.

'Singing and murmuring in your feastful mirth,
Joying to feel yourself alive;
Lord over Nature, Lord of the visible Earth,
Lord of the senses five.'

My quotation was hardly out of my lips before we had rounded the corner above the Convent; and a few yards further on could see across to Sanjowlie. In the centre of the level road stood the black and white liveries, the yellow-panelled 'rickshaw, and Mrs Keith-Wessington. I pulled up, looked, rubbed my eyes, and, I believe, must have said something. The next thing I knew was that I was lying face downward on the road, with Kitty kneeling above me in tears.

'Has it gone, child?' I gasped. Kitty only wept more bitterly.

'Has what gone, Jack dear? What does it all mean? There must be a mistake somewhere, Jack. A hideous mistake.' Her last words brought me to my feet—mad—raving for the time being.

'Yes, there *is* a mistake somewhere,' I repeated, 'a hideous mistake. Come and look at It.'

I have an indistinct idea that I dragged Kitty by the wrist along the road up to where It stood, and implored her for pity's sake to speak to It; to tell It that we were betrothed; that neither Death nor Hell could break the tie between us: and Kitty only knows how much more to the same effect. Now and again I appealed passionately to the Terror in the 'rickshaw to bear witness to all I had said, and to release me from a torture that was killing me. As I talked I suppose I must have told Kitty of my old relations with Mrs Wessington, for I saw her listen intently with a white face and blazing eyes.

'Thank you, Mr Pansay,' she said, 'that's *quite* enough. Syce, *ghora lao.*'

The syces, impassive as Orientals always are, had come up with the recaptured horses; and as Kitty sprang into her saddle I caught hold of her bridle, entreating her to hear me out and forgive. My answer was the cut of her riding-whip across my face from mouth to eye, and a word or two of farewell that even now I cannot write down. So I judged and judged rightly, that Kitty knew all; and I staggered back to the side of the 'rickshaw. My face was cut and bleeding, and the blow of the riding-whip had raised a livid blue wheal on it. I had no self-respect. Just then, Heatherlegh, who must have been following Kitty and me at a distance, cantered up.

'Doctor,' I said, pointing to my face, 'here's Miss Mannering's signature to my order of dismissal and I'll thank you for that lakh as soon as convenient.'

Heatherlegh's face, even in my abject miser, moved me to laughter.

'I'll stake my professional reputation,' he began.

'Don't be a fool,' I whispered. 'I've lost my life's happiness and you'd better take me home.'

As I spoke the 'rickshaw was gone. Then I lost all knowledge of what was passing. The crest of Jakko seemed to heave and roll like the crest of a cloud and fall in upon me.

Seven days later (on 7 May, that is to say) I was aware that I was lying in Heatherlegh's room as weak as a little child. Heatherlegh was watching me intently from behind the papers on his writing-table. His first words were not encouraging; but I was too far spent to be much moved by them.

'Here's Miss Kitty has sent back your letters. You corresponded a good deal, you young people. Here's a packet that looks like a ring and a cheerful sort of a note from Mannering Papa, which I've taken the liberty of reading and burning. The old gentleman's not pleased with you.'

'And Kitty?' I asked dully.

'Rather more drawn than her father from what she says. By the same token you must have been letting out any number of queer reminiscences just before I met you. Says that a man who would have behaved to a woman as you did to Mrs Wessington ought to kill himself out of sheer pity for his kind. She's a hot-headed little virago, your mash. Will have it too that you were suffering from D.T. when that row on the Jakko road turned up. Says she'll die before she ever speaks to you again.'

I groaned and turned over on the other side.

'Now you've got your choice, my friend. This engagement has to be broken off; and the Mannerings don't want to be too hard on you. Was it broken through D.T. or epileptic fits? Sorry

I can't offer you a better exchange unless you'd prefer hereditary insanity. Say the word and I'll tell 'em it's fits. All Simla knows about that scene on the Ladies' Mile. Come! I'll give you five minutes to think over it.'

During those five minutes I believe that I explored thoroughly the lowest circles of the inferno which man is permitted to tread on earth. And at the same time I was watching myself faltering through the dark labyrinths of doubt, misery and utter despair. I wondered, as Heatherlegh in his chair might have wondered, which dreadful alternative I should adopt. Presently I heard myself answering in a voice that I hardly recognized—

'They're confoundedly particular about morality in these parts. Give 'em fits, Heatherlegh, and my love. Now let me sleep a bit longer.'

Then my two selves joined, and it was only I (half-crazed, devil-driven I) that tossed in my bed tracing step by step the history of the past month.

'But I am in Simla,' I kept repeating to myself. 'I, Jack Pansay am in Simla, and there are no ghosts here. It's unreasonable of that woman to pretend there are. Why couldn't Agnes have left me alone? I never did her any harm. It might just as well have been me as Agnes. Only I'd never have come back on purpose to kill *her*. Why can't I be left alone—left alone and happy?'

It was high noon when I first awoke: and the sun was low in the sky before I slept—slept as the tortured criminal sleeps on his rack, too worn to feel further pain.

Next day I could not leave my bed. Heatherlegh told me in the morning that he had received an answer from Mr Mannering, and that, thanks to his (Heatherlegh's) friendly offices, the story of my affliction had travelled through the length and breadth of Simla, where I was on all sides much pitied.

'And that's rather more than you deserve,' he concluded pleasantly, 'though the Lord knows you've been going through a pretty severe mill. Never mind; we'll cure you yet, you perverse phenomenon.'

I declined firmly to be cured. 'You've been much too good to me already, old man,' said I; 'but I don't think I need trouble you further.'

In my heart I knew that nothing Heatherlegh could do would lighten the burden that had been laid upon me.

With that knowledge came also a sense of hopeless, impotent rebellion against the unreasonableness of it all. There were scores of men no better than I whose punishments had at least been reserved for another world; and I felt that it was bitterly, cruelly unfair that I alone should have been singled out for so hideous a fate. This mood would in time give place to another where it seemed that the 'rickshaw and I were the only realities in a world of shadows; that Kitty was a ghost; that Mannering, Heatherlegh, and all the other men and women I knew were all ghosts; and the great, grey hills themselves but vain shadows devised to torture me. From mood to mood I tossed backwards and forwards for seven weary days; my body growing daily stronger and stronger, until the bedroom looking-glass told me that I had returned to everyday life, and was as other men once more. Curiously enough my face showed no signs of the struggle I had gone through. It was pale indeed, but as expressionless and commonplace as ever. I had expected some permanent alteration—visible evidence of the disease that was eating me away. I found nothing.

On 15 May, I left Heatherlegh's house at eleven o'clock in the morning; and the instinct of the bachelor drove me to the club. There I found that every man knew my story as told by Heatherlegh, and was, in clumsy fashion, abnormally kind and attentive. Nevertheless, I recognized that for the rest of my natural life I should be among but not of my fellows; and I envied very bitterly indeed the laughing coolies on the Mall below. I lunched at the club, and at four o'clock wandered aimlessly down the Mall in the vague hope of meeting Kitty. Close to the Bandstand the black and white liveries joined me; and I heard Mrs Wessington's old appeal at my side. I had been expecting this ever since I came out; and was only surprised at her delay. The phantom 'rickshaw and I went side by side along the Chota Simla road in silence. Close to the bazar, Kitty and a man on horseback overtook and passed us. For any sign she gave I might have been a dog in the road. She did not even pay me the compliment of quickening her pace; though the rainy afternoon had served for an excuse.

So Kitty and her companion, and I and my ghostly Light-o'-Love, crept round Jakko in couples. The road was streaming with water; the pines dripped like roof-pipes on the rocks below, and the air was full of fine, driving rain. Two or three times I found myself saying to myself almost aloud: 'I'm Jack Pansay on leave at Simla—*at Simla!* Everyday, ordinary Simla. I mustn't forget that—I mustn't forget that.' Then I would try to recollect some of the gossip I had heard at the Club: the prices of so-and-so's horses—anything, in fact, that related to the work-a-day Anglo-Indian world I knew so well. I even repeated the multiplication table rapidly to myself, to make quite sure that I was not taking leave of my senses. It gave me much comfort; and must have prevented my hearing Mrs Wessington for a time.

Once more I wearily climbed the Convent slope and entered the level road. Here Kitty and the man started off at a canter, and I was left alone with Mrs Wessington. 'Agnes,' said I, 'will you put back your hood and tell me what it all means?' The hood dropped noiselessly, and I was face to face with my dead and buried mistress. She was wearing the dress in which I had last seen her alive; carried the same tiny handkerchief in her right hand; and the same card-case in her left. (A woman eight months dead with a card-case!) I had to pin myself down to the multiplication table, and to set both hands on the stone parapet of the road, to assure myself that that at least was real.

'Agnes,' I repeated, 'for pity's sake tell me what it all means.' Mrs Wessington leaned forward, with that odd, quick turn of the head I used to know so well, and spoke.

If my story had not already so madly overleaped the bounds of all human belief I should apologize to you now. As I know that no one—no, not even Kitty, for whom it is written as some sort of justification of my conduct—will believe me, I will go on. Mrs Wessington spoke and I walked with her from the Sanjowlie road to the turning below the Commander-in-Chief's house as I might walk by the side of any living woman's 'rickshaw, deep in conversation. The second and most tormenting of my moods of sickness had suddenly laid hold upon me, and like the prince in Tennyson's poem, 'I seemed to move amid a world of ghosts.' There had been a garden-party at the Commander-in-Chief's, and we two joined the crowd of homeward-bound folk. As I saw them it seemed that *they* were the shadows—impalpable fantastic shadows—that divided for Mrs Wessington's 'rickshaw to pass through. What we said during the course of that weird interview I cannot—indeed, I dare not—tell. Heatherlegh's comment would have been a short laugh and a remark that I had been 'mashing a brain-eye-and-stomach chimera'. It was a ghastly and, yet in some indefinable way, a marvellously dear experience. Could it be possible, I wondered, that I was in this life to woo a second time the woman I had killed by my own neglect and cruelty?

I met Kitty on the homeward road—a shadow among shadows. If I were to describe all the incidents of the next fortnight in their order, my story would never come to an end; and your patience would be exhausted. Morning after morning and evening after evening the ghostly 'rickshaw and I used to wander through Simla together. Wherever I went the four black and white liveries followed me and bore me company to and from my hotel. At the theatre I found them amid the crowd of yelling jhampanies; outside the club verandah, after a long evening of whist; at the Birthday Ball, waiting patiently for my reappearance; and in broad daylight when I went calling. Save that it cast no shadow, the 'rickshaw was in every respect as real to look upon as one of wood and iron. More than once, indeed, I have had to check myself from warning some hard-riding friend against cantering over it. More than once I have walked down the Mall deep in conversation with Mrs Wessington to the unspeakable amazement of the passers-by.

Before I had been out and about a week I learned that the 'fit' theory had been discarded in favour of insanity. However, I made no change in my mode of life. I called, rode, and dined out as freely as ever. I had a passion for the society of my kind which I had never felt before; I hungered to be among the realities of life; and at the same time I felt vaguely unhappy when I had been separated too long from my ghostly companion. It would be almost impossible to describe my varying moods from 15 May up to today.

The presence of the 'rickshaw filled me by turns with horror, blind fear, a dim sort of pleasure, and utter despair. I dared not leave Simla; and I knew that my stay there was killing me. I knew, moreover, that it was my destiny to die slowly and a little every day. My only anxiety was to get the penance over as quietly as might be. Alternately, I hungered for a sight of Kitty, and watched her outrageous flirtations with my successor—to speak more accurately, my successors—with amused interest. She was as much out of my life as I was out of hers. By day I wandered with Mrs Wessington almost content. By night I implored Heaven to let me return to the world as I used to know it. Above all these varying moods lay the sensation of dull, numbing wonder that the seen and the unseen should mingle so strangely on this earth to hound one poor soul to its grave.

August, 27—Heatherlegh has been indefatigable in his attendance on me; and only yesterday told me that I ought to send in an application for sick leave. An application to escape the company of a phantom! A request that the government would graciously permit me to get rid of five ghosts and an airy 'rickshaw by going to England! Heatherlegh's proposition moved me to almost hysterical laughter. I told him that I should await the end quietly at Simla; and I am sure that the end is not far off. Believe me that I dread its advent more than any word can say; and I torture myself nightly with a thousand speculations as to the manner of my death. Shall I die in my bed decently and as an English gentleman should die; or, in one last walk on the Mall, will my soul be wrenched from me to take its place forever and ever by the side of that ghastly phantasm? Shall I return to my old lost allegiance in the next world, or shall I meet Agnes loathing her and bound to her side through all eternity? Shall we two hover over the scene of our lives till the end of time? As the day of my death draws nearer, the intense horror that all living flesh feels toward escaped spirits from beyond the grave grows more and more powerful. It is an awful thing to go down quick among the dead with scarcely one-half of our life completed. It is a thousand times more awful to wait as I do in your midst, for I know not what unimaginable terror. Pity me, at least on the score of my 'delusion', for I know you will never believe what I have written here. Yet as surely as ever a man was done to death by the Powers of Darkness, I am that man. In justice, too, pity her. For as surely as ever a woman was killed by a man, I killed Mrs Wessington. And the last portion of my punishment is even now upon me.

NIGHT OF THE MILLENNIUM

Ruskin Bond

Jackals howled dismally, foraging for bones and offal down in the khud below the butcher's shop. Pasand was unperturbed by the sound. A robust young computer whiz-kid and patriotic multinational, he prided himself on being above and beyond all superstitious fears of the unknown. In his lexicon, the unknown was just something that was waiting to be discovered. Hence this walk, past the old cemetery late at night.

Midnight would see the new millennium in. The year 2000 beckoned, full of bright prospects for well-heeled young men like Pasand. True, there were millions—soon to be over a billion—sweating it out in the heat and dust of the plains below, scraping together a meagre living for themselves and their sprawling families. Not for them the advantages of a public school education, three cars in the garage, and a bank account in Bermuda. Ah well, mused Pasand, not everyone could have the brains and good luck, as well as inherited family wealth of course, that had made life so pleasant and promising for him. This was going to be the century in which the smart-asses would get to the top and all other varieties of asses would sink to the bottom. It was important to have a ruling elite, according to his philosophy; only then could slaves prosper!

He looked at his watch. It was just past midnight. He had eaten well, and he was enjoying his little walk along the lonely winding road which took him past the houses of the rich and famous, the Lais, the Banerjees, the Kapoors, the Ramchandanis— he was as good as any of them! Better, in fact. He was approaching his own personal Everest, while they had reached theirs and were on the downward slope, or so he presumed.

Here was the cemetery with its broken old tombstones, some of them dating from a hundred and fifty years ago: pathetic reminders of a once-powerful empire, now reduced to dust and crumbling monuments. Here lay colonels and magistrates, merchants and memsahibs, and many small children; fragile lives which had been snuffed out in more turbulent times. To Pasand, they were losers, all of them. He had nothing but contempt for those who hadn't been able to hang on to their power and glory. No lost empires for him!

The road here was very dark, for the trees grew thick on the northern slopes. Pasand felt a twinge of nervousness, but he was reassured by the feel of the cellphone in his pocket—he could always summon his driver or his armed bodyguard to come and pick him up.

The moon had risen over Nag Tibba, and the graves stood out in serried rows, as though forming a guard of honour for this modern knight in t-shirt and designer jeans. Through the deodars he saw a faint light on the perimeter of the cemetery. Here, he had learnt from one of his chamchas, lived a widow with a brood of small children. Although in poor health, she was still young and comely, and known to be lavish with her favours to those who were generous with their purses; for she needed the money for her hungry family.

She was also a little mad, they said, and preferred to sleep in one of the old domed tombs rather than in the quarters provided for her late husband, who had been the caretaker.

This did not bother Pasand. He was in search of sensual pleasure, not romance. And right now he felt an urgent need to exert his dominance over someone, preferably a woman, for he had to prove his manhood in some way. So far, most young women had shied away from his vainglorious and clumsy approach.

This woman wasn't young. She was in her late thirties, and poverty, malnutrition and ill-use had made her look much older. But there were vestiges of beauty in her smouldering eyes and sinewy limbs. Her gypsy blood must have had something to do with it. Her teeth gleamed in the darkness as she smiled at Pasand and invited him into her boudoir—the spacious tomb that she favoured most.

Pasand had no time for tender love-play. Clumsily, he clawed at her breasts but found they were not much larger than his own. He tore at her already tattered clothes, pressed his mouth hungrily to her dry lips. She made no attempt to resist. He had his way. Then, while he lay supine across the cold damp slab of a grave that covered the remains of some long-dead warrior, she leaned over him and bit him on the cheek and neck.

He cried out in pain and astonishment, and tried to sit up. But a number of hands, small but strong, thrust him back against the tombstone. Small mouths, sharp teeth, pressed against his flesh. Muddy fingers tore at his clothes. Those young teeth bit— and bit again. His screams mingled with the cries of the jackals.

'Patience, my children, patience,' crooned the woman. 'There is more than enough for all of you.'

They feasted.

Down in the ravine, the jackals started howling again, awaiting their turn. The bones would be theirs. Only the cellphone would be rejected.

THE WHITE TIGER

Alice Perrin

He was called the White Tiger by the villagers of the district because his yellow skin was pale with age, and his stripes so faded and far apart as to be almost invisible.

Having grown too large and heavy for cattle-killing with any ease, he had lately become a man-eater, and terrible were the stories told by those who had seen him and escaped the fatal blow of his huge paw. He was described as being the size of a bull-buffalo, with a belly that reached the ground, and a white moon between his ears, true tokens of the man-eater, as every native of India knows. He was said to have the power of assuming different shapes, and to lure his prey by the imitation of a human voice, and certainly his craft and cunning were such that not even Mar Singh, the local shikaree, had ever been able to trap him, or obtain a shot at him with his famous match-lock gun. And, Mar Singh had seen the tiger often, knew his favourite haunts and lairs, and could point out the very trees upon which he preferred to sharpen his murderous claws.

The brute continued to levy his terrible tax on the scanty population of a remote district, until the women and children were afraid to leave the village, and the men went out to work in the fields fearing for their lives.

At last, the increasing number of victims attracted the attention of the local authorities, and a reward of a hundred rupees was placed on the head of the White Tiger, with the result that Mar Singh, who clothed himself in khaki with a disreputable turban to match, and was regarded in his village as the wariest of hunters, redoubled his efforts to bring about the destruction of this awful scourge. Also, now that the fame of the White Tiger's misdeeds had penetrated to the headquarters, it was more than likely that a party of 'sahibs' would appear on the scene with elephants and rifles, in which case, though the tiger would be doomed, the reward would be distributed amongst the mahouts and the heaters, and Mar Singh himself would only receive a share.

So, night after night he perched on the branches of the trees above the favourite routes of the enemy, and from sunrise to sunset he haunted the outskirts of the jungle, and hung about the drinking-pools in the bed of the shrinking river, for, (unlike his cattle and game-killing brothers) the man-eater may be sought for at all hours. But to no purpose, the White Tiger seized a plump human victim once every few days, and Mar Singh's vision of the reward grew faint.

'The striped one is surely an evil spirit, and no beast at all!' said Mar Singh, who never uttered the word tiger if he could help it, for fear of ill-luck.

He had come in weary and crestfallen from a long day's search, having actually caught a glimpse of the White Tiger, and followed the tracks of the huge, square pugs to the edge of a thorny thicket, without the chance of a shot that could have taken effect; and he was pouring out his irritation and disgust to Kowta, his half-brother, who sat at the door of the family hovel contentedly smoking a hookah.

'Without doubt,' agreed Kowta, 'and therefore, would it not be wiser to let the sahib slay the Evil One if he be able?'

'What sahib?' asked Mar Singh sharply, pausing in the act of cleaning the precious match-lock gun, which was the envy and admiration of the village.

'Then thou has not heard the news?' said Kowta, innocently. 'A sahib has pitched his camp within one day's march of the village, and they say he has come to hunt the White Devil.'

The dreaded blow had fallen, and Mar Singh danced with rage.

'I will give him no news of the tiger. I will tell him nothing, and see, too, that thou remainest silent, Kowta, when he sends for information, else it will be the worse for thee!'

Kowta twiddled his big toe in the dust, always a sign of hesitation with a native, and Mar Singh scented trouble. He knew that Kowta was heavily in debt to the village usurer, and that sahibs often paid well for news of a tiger's movements. He was also aware that Kowta was jealous of his standing and reputation in the village, which would be increased ten-fold could he but destroy the tiger and earn the magnificent reward.

He changed his tone.

'See, brother,' he began insinuatingly, 'the utmost that the sahib would give thee might, perehance, be ten rupees, and thy share of the Government reward would scarcely be more than two. What are twelve rupees compared with forty, added to half the whiskers and claws of the Evil One, and perhaps, the lucky bone as well? All this will I give thee when I slay the beast, as I most assuredly must do if the sahib doth not interfere.'

Kowta puffed stolidly at his hookah and was maddeningly silent.

'Also,' continued Mar Singh, eagerly, 'consider the trouble that a sahib's camp brings upon a village. His servants, being rascals, will order supplies in the name of the sahib, and pay us nothing for them, and the police will annoy us if we complain. We shall be forced to beat the jungle, and many will be hurt and some killed, if not by the tiger then by other wild beasts, also?—'

'But how am I to tell that thou wilt give me the forty rupees and half the claws and whiskers? Whereas, a sahib holds to his promises, as we all know.'

'I swear it!' cried Mar Singh with fervour, 'by the skin of the White Devil I swear to deal well by thee!'

So, after some further argument, Kowta reluctantly agreed to take his brother's side, and Mar Singh unfolded a scheme by which Kowta was to proceed to the tents of the unwelcome Englishman, and pose as the shikaree of the district, possessing an intimate knowledge of the tiger's habits. Mar Singh would keep Kowta well-informed as to the movements of the tiger through the medium of the postman who ran from village to village with news and letters, and the sahib, at all hazards, was to be led in the wrong directions, until he grew weary of the fruitless chase, and withdrew from the district with his camp and elephants.

Kowta, therefore, proceeded to don the khaki costume, which he had long coveted, and the next morning he started on his diplomatic errand, while Mar Singh betook himself to the jungle to watch the movements of the White Tiger, that he might warn Kowta by the evening runner as to which locality must be avoided the following day.

Kowta enjoyed himself immensely at the camp. He arrived at sundown, and was interviewed by the sahib himself, to whom he gave voluble, but entirely false, information concerning the tiger, and promised to lead him direct to the animal's lair in the morning. The sahib, being young and new to the country, retired to bed in happy anticipation, and Kowta repaired to the kitchen tent, where, surrounded by the servants, he sat smoking his hookah and relating blood-curdling tales of the doings of the White Tiger.

Natives seldom sleep till far on in the night, and therefore, the gathering was at its height when the jingle of bells told of the postman's approach, and Kowta, explaining to the company that he was expecting news of his dying grandmother, went out into the moonlight to meet him. The chink-chink of the bunch of bells grew louder, and mingled with the regular grunts of the runner, and Kowta, stepping-forward into the sandy path, checked the man's rapid trot.

'Oh, brother!' he saluted, 'what word from Mar Singh, shikaree?'

'Kowta, there is no word from the mouth of Mar Singh, thy brother, seeing that but an hour after thy departure he was slain by the White Tiger on the outskirts of the grazing plain, and Merijhan, the cow-herd, saw it happen. I bring the evil news to thee fresh from thy village.'

For a moment Kowta was paralysed by the horror of the dreadful and unexpected news. Then he asked questions, and learned that his brother's body had been recovered by a party of villagers who had sallied forth with drums and fireworks and had driven the beast from its prey. The mangled remains now lay in the family hut, and Kowta's presence was required to make arrangements for the funeral.

Kowta slipped some coppers into the postman's willing hand, and charged him to keep silence as to the catastrophe when delivering letters in the camp. Then he collected his belongings, and left a plausible message for the sahib to say he had been summoned to his grandmother's deathbed, but would return with all haste the following day. He set out in the moonlight along the narrow jungle path, bordered by tall grass higher than his head, and walked rapidly, though the heat was over-powering, until, just as the dawn broke, he came within sight of the village. He strode through the fields of tobacco and young wheat, and saw the bright green parrots flashing to and fro in the vivid yellow light; partridges ran from beneath his feet, calling shrilly as they disappeared behind the clumps of dry grass; and he could hear the jungle fowl in the distance crowing to the rising sun. Everything was awake and glowing with life, and the dark interior of the hut, where the women were wailing and the atmosphere seemed charged with death, formed a sharp contrast to the outside world.

The mangled body of the dead man, torn and chewed by the tiger, lay on the string bedstead, surrounded by a noisy group of mourning relatives. There was nothing for Kowta to do but arrange for the remains to be taken to the burning-ground in the evening and to attempt to pacify the wailing throng, until, as the fierce, hot noon came on, they gradually dispersed, and even the widow of the dead man sought a siesta in a neighbour's hut, while Kowta sat down on the threshold of his home to think.

An idea had been slowly forming in his brain which brought with it a wave of exultation. Why should not he compass the destruction of the White Tiger, and so earn the whole reward. He was in debt to the moneylender, and he also greatly desired a plot of land that was for sale just outside the village, and the hundred rupees would not only free him from debt, but would also purchase the coveted little piece of ground. It was true that Mar Singh himself had never succeeded in shooting the White Tiger, but then his difficulty had always been the want of suitable bait, whereas *now*—Kowta glanced back into the shadow of the hut and shivered, remembering the native belief that the soul of the tiger's victim becomes the servant of the slayer, and is bound to warn the master when danger threatens.

Mar Singh's spirit might or might not be in bondage to the White Tiger, but, in any case, the hundred rupees was worth some risk, and with proper precautions there should be little or no danger, seeing that the match-lock gun had been recovered uninjured. Kowta rose and looked up and down the little village street. Not a breeze stirred the giant leaves of the plantain trees, not a bird uttered a note, not a voice broke the breathless calm, every creature except himself was wrapped in slumber.

He made up his mind. He would attempt the plan, and afterwards, whether he succeeded or failed, he could deny all knowledge of the disappearance of his brother's body, and encourage the suggestion which would naturally arise, that the sorcery of the White Tiger had spirited the corpse away. So, he gathered the wreck of Mar Singh into a bundle, wrapping it in his own white cotton-waste waist-cloth, and with the loaded match-lock over his shoulder, went swiftly through the sleeping village and out into the fields, invoking on his errand the blessing of Durga, the goddess who rides the tiger. Thence, he took a narrow jungle path with tangled shrubs closing over his head, and as he emerged from this on to the bushy, broken ground leading to the river, he gathered a leaf from the nearest tree and muttered—

'As thy life has departed, so may the striped one die.'

He walked up the pebbly bed of the dwindling stream till

he reached a pool of clear water, in the wet margin of which were printed countless tracks of animals that had drunk there during the night. Wild pig, jackal, fox, hyena, all had statiated their thirst, but the White Tiger had not been of the company. A hundred yards off lay another pool, and around it Kowta found a solitary track—the big, square pugs of the beast who, by common consent of the other jungle inhabitants, had been given a wide berth, and allowed to drink alone.

The marks were not more than a few hours old, and Kowta followed them cautiously, grasping the gun and dragging his other burden behind him along the gravelly sand. The footprints led him to some rocky boulders, on the summit of which a family of monkeys sat peacefully hunting for fleas, a sign that the tiger was not on the move, else they would have been crashing and chattering in the nearest trees, and pouring forth torrents of abuse. The pugs led on round the rocks to a shady thicket of thorn bushes in a deep ravine, and Kowta felt that he had tracked the White Tiger to his lair.

He laid his brother's body close to the edge of the thorny thicket, and then cast about for a safe retreat within easy shot, but no climbable trees were at hand, the cover consisting of low, scrubby bushes. The only suitable place of concealment seemed to be the nearest rock, behind which it would be easy to hide and yet command a good view of the bait.

The odour of the dead body tainted the air as the sun blazed full upon it, which suited Kowta's purpose well, for tigers prefer their food as carrion, and hunger would soon bring the beast forth. Kowta lay down behind the rock and waited. A hot, high wind was blowing, and the sand from the riverbed, getting into his eyes, made them smart, but he paid no heed to the discomfort, and only watched the thicket intently for the least movement.

He held his breath when, presently, something rustled and crept out—merely a mangy little jackal with loosely-hanging brush, who sprang four feet into the air as he came suddenly on Mar Singh's body. Then the animal uttered the long, miserable wail known as the 'pheeaow cry,' and ran back into the thicket, causing Kowta's heart to beat high with hope, for he knew the jackal was a 'provider', one that gives notice to the tiger when food is to be found.

Now, without doubt the Evil One would steal forth, and nothing could then prevent a shot at such close quarters taking effect. A pea-fowl screeched wildly, and Kowta could hear the agitated flapping of its wings, that also was a token that the tiger moved. The monkeys set up a clatter and scuttled from the rocks. He was coming—the White Devil, the evil-striped one!

Kowta waited breathless, his pulses throbbing in his ears, thinking of the hundred rupees and the plot of ground that were now almost his own, and gazing fixedly over the sickening, twisted limbs of the mutilated body only a few yards from him.

The tension was terrible, and the cracking of a dry twig behind him sounded almost like the report of a gun, he felt a surging in his brain, and, as another stick snapped, some irresistible power compelled him to turn his head.

There, five yards behind him, crouched the White Tiger, that with silent steps and awful cunning had stalked him from the village. The ears were flattened to the broad head, the long white whiskers bristled and quivered, the wicked yellow eyes glared, and held the man helpless, spellbound with horror, waiting for the spring that came with a hissing, growling roar, as the White Tiger claimed yet another victim.

THE DOCTOR'S GHOST

Dr Norman Macleod

A friend of mine, a medical man, once went on a fishing expedition with an old college acquaintance, an army surgeon, whom he had not met for many years, from his having been in India with his regiment. McDonald, the army surgeon, was a thorough Highlander, and slightly tinged with what is called the superstition of his countrymen, and at the time I speak of was liable to rather depressed spirits from an unsound liver. His native air was, however, rapidly renewing his youth; and when he and his old friend paced along the banks of the fishing stream in a lonely part of Argyllshire, and sent their lines like airy gossamers over the pools, and touched the water over a salmon's nose, so temptingly that the best-principled and wisest fish could not resist the bite, McDonald had apparently regained all his buoyancy of spirit.

They had been fishing together for about a week with great success, when McDonald proposed to pay a visit to a family with which he was acquainted, that would separate him from his friend for some days. But whenever he spoke of their intended separation, he sank down into his old gloomy state, at one time declaring that he felt as if they were never to meet again. My friend tried to rally him, but in vain. They parted at the trouting stream, McDonald's route being across a mountain pass, with which, however, he had been well acquainted in his youth, though the road was lonely and wild in the extreme.

The doctor returned early in the evening to his resting-place, which was a shepherd's house lying on the very outskirts of the 'settlements,' and beside a foaming mountain stream. The shepherd's only attendants at the time were two herd lads and three dogs. Attached to the hut, and communicating with it by a short passage, was rather a comfortable room which 'the Laird' had fitted up to serve as a sort of lodge for himself in the midst of his shooting-ground, and which he had put for a fortnight at the disposal of my friend.

Shortly after sunset on the day I mention the wind began to rise suddenly to a gale, the rain descended in torrents, and the night became extremely dark. The shepherd seemed uneasy, and several times went to the door to inspect the weather. At last he roused the fears of the doctor for McDonald's safety, by expressing the hope that by this time he was 'owre that awfu' black moss, and across the red burn.'

Every traveller in the Highlands knows how rapidly these mountain streams rise, and how confusing the moor becomes in a dark night. The confusion of memory once a doubt is suggested, the utter mystery of places, becomes, as I know from experience, quite indescribable.

'The black moss and red burn' were words that were never after forgot by the doctor, from the strange feelings they produced when first heard that night; for there came into his mind terrible thoughts and forebodings about poor McDonald, and reproaches for never having considered his possible danger in attempting such a journey alone. In vain the shepherd assured him that he must have reached a place of safety before the darkness and the storm came on. A presentiment which he could not cast off made him so miserable that he could hardly refrain from tears. But nothing could be done to relieve the anxiety now become so painful.

The doctor at last retired to bed about midnight. For a long time he could not sleep. The raging of the stream below the small window, and the thuds of the storm, made him feverish and restless. But at last he fell into a sound and dreamless sleep. Out of this, however, he was suddenly roused by a peculiar noise in his room, not very loud, but utterly indescribable. He heard tap, tap, tap at the window, and he knew, from the relation which the wall of the room bore to the rock, that the glass could not be touched by human hand.

After listening for a moment, and forcing himself to smile at his nervousness, he turned round, and began again to seek repose. But now a noise began too near and loud to make sleep possible. Starting and sitting up in bed, he heard repeated in rapid succession, as if someone was spitting in anger, and close to his bed,—'Fit! Fit! Fit!' and then a prolonged 'whir-r-r' from another part of the room, while every chair began to move, and the table to jerk!

The doctor remained in breathless silence, with every faculty intensely acute. He frankly confessed that he heard his heart beating, for the sound was so unearthly, so horrible, and something seemed to come so near him, that he began seriously to consider whether or not he had some attack of fever which affected his brain—for, remember, he had not tasted a drop of the shepherd's small store of whisky! He felt his pulse, composed his spirits, and compelled himself to exercise calm judgment.

Straining his eyes to discover anything, he plainly saw at last a white object moving, but without sound, before him. He knew that the door was shut and the window also.

An overpowering conviction then seized him, which he could not resist, that his friend McDonald was dead! By an effort he seized a lucifer-box on a chair beside him, and struck a light. No white object could be seen. The room appeared to be as when he went to bed. The door was shut. He looked at his watch, and particularly marked that the hour was twenty-two minutes past three. But the match was hardly extinguished when, louder than ever, the same unearthly cry of 'Fit! Fit! Fit!' was heard, followed by the same horrible whir-r-r-r, which made his teeth chatter. Then the movement of the table and every chair in the room was resumed with increased violence, while the tapping on the window was heard above the storm. There was no bell in the room, but the doctor, on hearing all this frightful confusion of sounds again repeated, and beholding the white object moving towards him in terrible silence, began to thump the wooden partition and to shout at the top of his voice for the shepherd, and having done so, he dived his head under the blankets!

The shepherd soon made his appearance, in his night-shirt, with a small oil-lamp, or 'crusey,' over his head, anxiously inquiring as he entered the room:

'What is't, doctor? What's wrang? Pity me, are ye ill?'

'Very!' cried the doctor. But before he could give any explanation a loud whir-r-r was heard, with the old cry of 'Fit!' close to the shepherd, while two chairs fell at his feet! The shepherd sprang back, with a half scream of terror the lamp was dashed to the ground, and the door violently shut.

'Come back!' shouted the doctor. 'Come back, Duncan,

instantly, I command you!'

The shepherd opened the door very partially, and said, in terrified accents:

'Gude be aboot us, that was awfu'! What under heaven is't?'

'Heaven knows, Duncan,' ejaculated the doctor with agitated voice, 'but do pick up the lamp, and I shall strike a light.'

Duncan did so in no small fear; but as he made his way to the bed in the darkness to get a match from the doctor, something caught his foot; he fell; and then, amidst the same noises and tumults of chairs, which immediately filled the apartment, the 'Fit! Fit! Fit! Fit!' was prolonged with more vehemence than ever!

The doctor sprang up, and made his way out of the room, but his feet were several times tripped by some unknown power, so that he had the greatest difficulty in reaching the door without a fall. He was followed by Duncan, and both rushed out of the room, shutting the door after them. A new light having been obtained, they both returned with extreme caution, and, it must be added, real fear, in the hope of finding some cause or other for all those terrifying signs.

Would it surprise our readers to hear that they searched the room in vain?—that, after minutely examining under the table, chairs, bed, everywhere, and with the door shut, not a trace could be found of anything? Would they believe that they heard during the day how poor McDonald had staggered, half dead from fatigue, into his friend's house, and falling into a fit, had died at *twenty-two minutes past three* that morning? We do not ask anyone to accept of all this as true. But we pledge our honour to the following facts:

The doctor, after the day's fishing was over, had packed his rod so as to take it into his bedroom; but he had left a minnow attached to the hook. A white cat left in the room swallowed the minnow and was hooked. The unfortunate gourmand had vehemently protested against this intrusion into its upper lip by the violent 'Fit! Fit! Fit!' with which she tried to spit the hook out; the reel added the mysterious whir-r-r-r; and the disengaged line, getting entangled in the legs of the chairs and table, as the hooked cat attempted to flee from her tormentor, set the furniture in motion, and tripped up both shepherd and doctor; while an ivy branch kept tapping at the window! Will anyone doubt the existence of ghosts and a spirit-world after this?

I have only to add that the doctor's skill was employed during the night in cutting the hook out of the cat's lip, while his poor patient, yet most impatient, was held by the shepherd in a bag, the head alone of the puss, with hook and minnow, being visible. McDonald made his appearance in a day or two, rejoicing once more to see his friend, and greatly enjoying the ghost story.

THURNLEY ABBEY

Perceval Landon

Three years ago I was on my way out to the East, and as an extra day in London was of some importance, I took the Friday evening mail-train to Brindisi instead of the usual Thursday morning Marseilles express. Many people shrink from the long forty-eight-hour train journey through Europe, and the subsequent rush across the Mediterranean on the nineteen-knot *Isis* or *Osiris*; but there is really very little discomfort on either the train or the mail-boat, and unless there is actually nothing for me to do, I always like to save the extra day and a half in London before I say goodbye to her for one of my longer tramps. This time—it was early, I remember, in the shipping season, probably about the beginning of September—there were few passengers, and I had a compartment in the P&O. Indian express to myself all the way from Calais. All Sunday I watched the blue waves dimpling the Adriatic, and the pale rosemary along the cuttings; the plain white towns, with their flat roofs and their hold 'duomos', and the grey-green gnarled olive orchards of Apulia. The journey was just like any other. We ate in the dining-car as often and as long as we decently could. We slept after luncheon; we dawdled the afternoon away with yellow-backed novels; sometimes we exchanged platitudes in the smoking-room, and it was there that I met Alastair Colvin.

Colvin was a man of middle height, with a resolute, well-cut jaw; his hair was turning grey; his moustache was sun-whitened, otherwise he was clean-shaven—obviously a gentleman, and obviously also a pre-occupied man. He had no great wit. When spoken to, he made the usual remarks in the right way, and I dare say he refrained from banalities only because he spoke less than the rest of us; most of the time he buried himself in the Wagon-lit Company's time-table, but seemed unable to concentrate his attention on any one page of it. He found that I had been over the Siberian railway, and for a quarter of an hour he discussed it with me. Then he lost interest in it, and rose to go to his compartment. But he came back again very soon, and seemed glad to pick up the conversation again.

Of course, this did not seem to me to be of any importance. Most travellers by train become a trifle infirm of purpose after thirty-six hours' rattling. But Colvin's restless way I noticed in somewhat marked contrast with the man's personal importance and dignity; especially ill-suited was it to his finely made large hand with strong, broad, regular nails and its few lines. As I looked at his hand I noticed a long, deep, and recent scar of ragged shape. However, it is absurd to pretend that I thought anything was unusual. I went off at five o'clock on Sunday afternoon to sleep away the hour or two that had still to be got through before we arrived at Brindisi.

Once there, we few passengers transhipped our hand baggage, verified our berths—there were only a score of us in all—and then, after an aimless ramble of half an hour in Brindisi, we returned to dinner at the Hotel International, not wholly surprised that the town had been the death of Virgil. If I remember rightly, there is a gaily painted hall at the International—I do not wish to advertise anything, but there is no other place in Brindisi at which to await the coming of the mails—and after dinner I was looking with awe at a trellis overgrown with blue vines, when Colvin moved across the room to my table. He picked up *Il Seculo*, but almost immediately gave up the pretence of reading it. He turned squarely to me and said:

'Would you do me a favour?'

One doesn't do favours to stray acquaintances on Continental expresses without knowing something more of them than I knew of Colvin. But I smiled in a noncommittal way, and asked him what he wanted. I wasn't wrong in part of my estimate of him; he said bluntly:

'Will you let me sleep in your cabin on the Osiris?' And he coloured a little as he said it.

Now, there is nothing more tiresome than having to put up with a stable-companion at sea, and I asked him rather pointedly:

'Surely, there is room for all of us?' I thought that perhaps he had been partnered off with some mangy Levantine, and wanted to escape from him at all hazards.

Colvin, still somewhat confused, said: 'Yes; I am in a cabin by myself. But you would do me the greatest favour if you would allow me to share yours.'

This was all very well, but, besides the fact that I always sleep better when alone, there had been some recent thefts on board English liners, and I hesitated, frank and honest and self-conscious as Colvin was. Just then the mail-train came in with a clatter and a rush of escaping steam, and I asked him to see me again about it on the boat when we started. He answered me curtly—I suppose he saw the mistrust in my manner? 'I am a member of White's.' I smiled to myself as he said it, but I remembered in a moment that the man—if he were really what he claimed to be, and I make no doubt that he was—must have been sorely put to it before he urged the fact as a guarantee of his respectability to a total stranger at a Brindisi hotel.

That evening, as we cleared the red and green harbour-lights of Brindisi, Colvin explained. This is his story in his own words.

'When I was travelling in India some years ago, I made the acquaintance of a youngish man in the Forests Service. We camped out together for a week, and I found him a pleasant companion. John Broughton was a light-hearted soul when off duty, but a steady and capable man in any of the small emergencies that continually arise in that department. He was liked and trusted by Indians and though a trifle over-pleased with himself when he escaped to civilisation at Simla or Calcutta, Broughton's future was well-assured in Government service, when a fair-sized estate was unexpectedly left to him, and he joyfully shook the dust to the Indian plains from his feet and returned to England. For five years he drifted about London. I saw him now and then. We dined together about every eighteen months, and I could trace pretty exactly the gradual sickening of Broughton with a merely idle life. He then set out on a couple of long voyages, returned as restless as before, and at last told me that he had decided to marry and settle down at his place, Thurnley Abbey, which had long been empty. He spoke about looking after the property and standing for his constituency in the usual way. Vivien Wilde, his *fiancée*, had, I suppose, begun to take him in hand. She was a pretty girl with a deal of fair hair and rather an exclusive manner; deeply religious in a narrow school, she was still kindly and high-spirited, and I thought that Broughton was in luck. He was quite happy and full of information about his future.

'Among other things, I asked him about Thurnley Abbey. He confessed that he hardly knew the place. The last tenant, a man called Clarke, had lived in one wing for fifteen years and seen no one. He had been a miser and a hermit. It was the rarest thing for alight to be seen at the Abbey after dark. Only the barest necessities of life were ordered, and the tenant himself received them at the side-door. His one half-caste manservant, after a month's stay in the house, had abruptly left without warning, and had returned to the Southern States. One thing Broughton complained bitterly about: Clarke had wilfully spread the rumour among the villagers that the Abbey was haunted, and had even condescended to play childish tricks with spirit-lamps and salt in order to scare trespassers away at night. He had been detected in the act of this tomfoolery, but the story spread, and no one, said Broughton, would venture near the house except in broad daylight. The hauntedness of Thurnley Abbey was now, he said with a grin, part of the gospel of the countryside, but he and his young wife were going to change all that. Would I propose myself any time I liked? I, of course, said I would, and equally, of course, intended to do nothing of the sort without a definite invitation.

'The house was put in thorough repair, though not a stick of the old furniture and tapestry were removed. Floors and ceilings were relaid: the roof was made watertight again, and the dust of half a century was scoured out. He showed me some photographs of the place. It was called an Abbey, though as a matter of fact it had been only the infirmary of the long-vanished Abbey of Closter some five miles away. The larger part of this building remained as it had been in pre-Reformation days, but a wing had been added in Jacobean times, and that part of the house had been kept in something like repair by Mr Clarke. He had in both the ground and first floors set a heavy timber door, strongly barred with iron, in the passage between the earlier and the Jacobean parts of the house, and had entirely neglected the former. So there had been a good deal of work to be done.

'Broughton, whom I saw in London two or three times about this period, made a deal of fun over the positive refusal of the workmen to remain after sundown. Even after the electric light had been put into every room, nothing would induce them to remain, though, as Broughton observed, electric light was death on ghosts. The legend of the Abbey's ghosts had gone far and wide, and the men would take no risks. They went home in batches of five and six, and even during the daylight hours there was an inordinate amount of talking between one and another, if either happened to be out of sight of his companion. On the whole, though nothing of any sort or kind had been conjured up even by their heated imaginations during their five months' work upon the Abbey, the belief in the ghosts was rather strengthened than otherwise in Thurnley because of the men's confessed nervousness, and local tradition declared itself in favour of the ghost of an immured nun.'

'Good old nun!' said Broughton.

'I asked him whether in general he believed in the possibility of ghosts, and, rather to my surprise, he said that he couldn't say he entirely disbelieved in them. A man in India had told him one morning in camp that he believed that his mother was dead in England, as her vision had come to his tent the night before. He had not been alarmed, but had said nothing, and the figure vanished again. As a matter of fact, the next possible dak-walla brought on a telegram announcing the mother's death. 'There the thing was,' said Broughton. But at Thurnley he was practical enough. He roundly cursed the idiotic selfishness of Clarke, Whose silly antics had caused all the inconvenience. At the same time, he couldn't refuse to sympathise to some extent with the ignorant workmen. 'My own idea,' said he, 'is that if a ghost ever does come in one's way, one ought to speak to it.'

'I agreed. Little as I knew of the ghost world and its conventions, I had always remembered that a spook was in honour bound to wait to be spoken to. It didn't seem much to do, and I felt that the sound of one's own voice would at any rate reassure oneself as to one's wakefulness. But there are few ghosts outside Europe—few, that is, that a white man can see—and I had never been troubled with any. However, as I have said, I told Broughton that I agreed.

'So the wedding took place, and I went to it in a tall hat which I bought for the occasion, and the new Mrs Broughton smiled very nicely at me afterwards. As it had to happen, I took the Orient Express that evening and was not in England again for nearly six months. Just before I came back I got a letter from Broughton. He asked if I could see him in London or come to Thurnley, as he thought I should be better able to help him than anyone else he knew. His wife sent a nice message to me at the end, so I was reassured about at least one thing. I wrote from Budapest that I would come and see him at Thurnley two days after my arrival in London, and as I sauntered out of the Pannonia into the Kerepesi Utcza to post my letters, I wondered of what earthly service I could be to Broughton. I had been out with him after tiger on foot, and I could imagine few men better able at a pinch to manage their own business. However, I had nothing to do, so after dealing with some small accumulations of business during my absence, I packed a kit-bag and departed to Euston.

'I was met by Broughton's great limousine at Thurnley Road station, and after a drive of nearly seven miles we echoed through the sleepy streets of Thurnley village, into which the main gates of the park thrust themselves, splendid with pillars and spread-eagles and tom-cats rampant atop of them. I never was a herald, but I know that the Broughtons have the right to supporters Heaven knows why! From the gates a quadruple avenue of beech trees led inwards for a quarter of a mile. Beneath them a neat strip of fine turf edged the road and ran back until the poison of the dead beech leaves killed it under the trees. There were many wheel-tracks on the road, and a comfortable little pony trap jogged past me laden with a country parson and his wife and daughter. Evidently there was some garden party going on at the Abbey. The road dropped away to the right at the end of the avenue, and I could see the Abbey across a wide pasturage and a broad lawn thickly dotted with guests.

'The end of the building was plain. It must have been almost mercilessly austere when it was first built, but time had crumbled the edges and toned the stone down to an orange-lichened grey wherever it showed behind its curtain of magnolia, jasmine, and ivy. Farther on was the three-storeyed Jacobean house, tall and handsome. There had not been the slightest attempt to adapt the one to the other, but the kindly ivy had glossed over the touching-point. There was a tall flèche in the middle of the building, surmounting a small bell tower. Behind the house there rose the mountainous verdure of Spanish chestnuts all the way up the hill.

'Broughton had seen me coming from afar, and walked across from his other guests to welcome me before turning me over to the butler's care. This man was sandy-haired and rather inclined to be talkative. He could, however, answer hardly any questions about the house; he had, he said, only been there three weeks. Mindful of what Broughton had told me, I made no inquiries about ghosts, though the room into which I was shown might have justified anything. It was a very large low room with oak beams projecting from the white ceiling. Every inch of the walls, including the doors, was covered with tapestry, and a remarkably fine Italian four post bedstead, heavily draped, added to the darkness and dignity of the place. All the furniture was old, well-made, and dark. Underfoot there was a plain green pile carpet, the only new thing about the room except the electric light fittings and the jugs and basins. Even the looking-glass on the dressing-table was an old pyramidal Venetian glass set in heavy repoussé frame of tarnished silver.

'After a few minutes' cleaning up, I went downstairs and out upon the lawn, where I greeted my hostess. The people gathered there were of the usual country type, all anxious to be pleased and roundly curious as to the new master of the Abbey. Rather to my surprise, and quite to my pleasure, I rediscovered Glenham, whom I had known well in old days in Barotseland: he lived quite close, as, he remarked with a grin, I ought to have known. 'But,' he added, 'I don't live in a place like this.' He swept his hand to the long, low lines of the Abbey in obvious admiration, and then, to my intense interest, muttered beneath his breath, 'Thank God!'. He saw that I had overheard him, and turning to me said decidedly, 'Yes, "thank God" I said, and I meant it. I wouldn't live at the Abbey for all Broughton's money.'

'But surely,' I demurred, 'you know that old Clarke was discovered in the very act of setting light to his bug-a-boos?'

'Glenham shrugged his shoulders. 'Yes, I know about that.

But there is something wrong with the place still. All I can say is that Broughton is a different man since he has lived here. I don't believe that he will remain much longer. But—you're staying here?—well, you'll hear all about it tonight. There's a big dinner, I understand.' The conversation turned off to old reminiscences, and Glenham soon after had to go.

'Before I went to dress that evening I had twenty minutes' talk with Broughton in his library. There was no doubt that the man was altered, gravely altered. He was nervous and fidgety, and I found him looking at me only when my eye was off him. I naturally asked him what he wanted of me. I told him I would do anything I could, but that I couldn't conceive what he lacked that I could provide. He said with a lustreless smile that there was, however, something, and that he would tell me the following morning. It struck me that he was somehow ashamed of himself. And perhaps ashamed of the part he was asking me to play. However, I dismissed the subject from my mind and went up to dress in my palatial room. As I shut the door a draught blew out the Queen of Sheba from the wall, and I noticed that the tapestries were not fastened to the wall at the bottom. I have always held very practical views about spooks, and it has often seemed to me that the slow waving in firelight of loose tapestry upon a wall would account for ninety-nine per cent of the stories one hears. Certainly, the dignified undulation of this lady with her attendants and huntsmen—one of whom was untidily cutting the throat of a fallow deer upon the very steps on which King Solomon, a grey-faced Flemish nobleman with the order of the Golden Fleece, awaited his fair visitor—gave colour to my hypothesis.

'Nothing much happened at dinner. The people were very much like those of the garden party. A young woman next me seemed anxious to know what was being read in London. As she was far more familiar than I with the most recent magazines and literary supplements, I found salvation in being myself instructed in the tendencies of modern fiction. All true art, she said, was shot through and through with melancholy. How vulgar were the attempts at wit that marked so many modern books! From the beginning of literature it had always been tragedy that embodied the highest attainment of every age. To call such works morbid merely begged the question. No thoughtful man—she looked sternly at me through the steel rim of her glasses—could fail to agree with me. Of course, as one would, I immediately and properly said that I slept with Pett Ridge and Jacobs under my pillow at night, and that if *Jorrocks* weren't quite so large and cornery, I would add him to the company. She hadn't read any of them, so I was saved—for a time. But I remember grimly that she said that the dearest wish of her life was to be in some awful and soul-freezing situation of horror, and I remember that she dealt hardly with the hero of Nat Paynter's vampire story, between nibbles at her brown-bread ice. She was a cheerless soul, and I couldn't help thinking that if there were many such in the neighbourhood, it was not surprising that old Glenham had been stuffed with some nonsense or the other about the Abbey. Yet, nothing could well have been less creepy than the glitter of silver and glass, and the subdued lights and cackle of conversation all round the dinner-table.

'After the ladies had gone I found myself talking to the rural dean. He was a thin, earnest man, who at once turned the conversation to old Clarke's buffooneries. But, he said, Mr Broughton had introduced such a new and cheerful spirit, not only into the Abbey, but, he might say, into the whole neighbourhood, that he had great hopes that the ignorant superstitions of the past were from henceforth destined to oblivion. Thereupon his other neighbour, a portly gentleman of independent means and position, audibly remarked 'Amen', which damped the rural dean, and we talked of partridges past, partridges present, and pheasants to come. At the other end of the table Broughton sat with a couple of his friends, red-faced hunting men. Once I noticed that they were discussing me, but I paid no attention to it at the time. I remembered it a few hours later.

'By eleven all the guests were gone, and Broughton, his wife, and I were alone together under the fine plaster ceiling of the Jacobean drawing-room. Mrs Broughton talked about one or two of the neighbours, and then, with a smile, said that she knew I would excuse her, shook hands with me, and went off to bed. I am not very good at analysing things, but I felt that she talked a little uncomfortably and with a suspicion of effort, smiled rather conventionally, and was obviously glad to go. These things seem trifling enough to repeat, but I had throughout the faint feeling that everything was not square. Under the circumstances, this was enough to set me wondering what on earth the service could be that I was to render—wondering also whether the whole business were not some ill-advised jest in order to make me come down from London for a mere shooting-party.

'Broughton said little after she had gone. But he was evidently labouring to bring the conversation round to the so-called haunting of the Abbey. As soon as I saw this, of course I asked him directly about it. He then seemed at once to lose interest in the matter. There was no doubt about it: Broughton was somehow a changed man, and to my mind he had changed in no way for the better. Mrs Broughton seemed no sufficient cause. He was clearly very fond of her, and she of him. I reminded him that he was going to tell me what I could do for him in the morning, pleaded my journey, lighted a candle, and went upstairs with him. At the end of the passage leading into the old house he grinned weakly and said, 'Mind, if you see a ghost, do talk to it; you said you would.' He stood irresolutely a moment and then turned away. At the door of his dressing-room he paused once more: 'I'm here,' he called out, 'if you should want anything. Good night,' and he shut his door.

'I went along the passage to my room, undressed, switched on a lamp beside my bed, read a few pages of *The Jungle Book*, and then, more than ready for sleep, turned the light off and went fast asleep.

'Three hours later I woke up. There was not a breath of wind outside. There was not even a flicker of light from the fireplace. As I lay there, an ash tinkled slightly as it cooled, but there was hardly a gleam of the dullest red in the grate. An owl cried among the silent Spanish chestnuts on the slope outside. I idly reviewed the events of the day, hoping that I should fall off to sleep again before I reached dinner. But at the end I seemed as wakeful as ever. There was no help for it. I must read my *Jungle Book* again till I felt ready to go off, so I fumbled for the pear at the end of the cord that hung down inside the bed, and I switched on the bedside lamp. The sudden glory dazzled me for a moment. I felt under my pillow for my book with half-shut eyes. Then, growing used to the light, I happened to look down to the foot of my bed.

'I can never tell you really what happened then. Nothing I could ever confess in the most abject words could even faintly picture to you what I felt. I know that my heart stopped dead, and my throat shut automatically. In one instinctive movement

I crouched back up against the head-boards of the bed, staring at the horror. The movement set my heart going again, and the sweat dripped from every pore. I am not a particularly religious man, but I had always believed that God would never allow any supernatural appearance to present itself to man in such a guise and in such circumstances that harm, either bodily or mental, could result to him. I can only tell you that at that moment both my life and my reason rocked unsteadily on their seats.'

The other *Osiris* passengers had gone to bed. Only he and I remained leaning over the starboard railing, which rattled uneasily now and then under the fierce vibration of the over-engined mail-boat. Far over, there were the lights of a few fishing-smacks riding out the night, and a great rush of white combing and seething water fell out and away from us overside.

At last Colvin went on:

'Leaning over the foot of my bed, looking at me, was a figure swathed in a rotten and tattered veiling. This shroud passed over the head, but left both eyes and the right side of the face bare. It then followed the line of the arm down to where the hand grasped the bed-end. The face was not entirely that of a skull, though the eyes and the flesh of the face were totally gone. There was a thin, dry skin drawn tightly over the features, and there was some skin left on the hand. One wisp of hair crossed the forehead. It was perfectly still. I looked at it, and it looked at me, and my brains turned dry and hot in my head. I had still got the pear of the electric lamp in my hand, and I played idly with it; only I dared not turn the light out again. I shut my eyes, only to open them in a hideous terror the same second. The thing had not moved. My heart was thumping, and the sweat cooled me as it evaporated. Another cinder tinkled in the grate, and a panel creaked in the wall.

'My reason failed me. For twenty minutes, or twenty seconds, I was able to think of nothing else but this awful figure, till there came, hurtling through the empty channels of my senses, the remembrance that Broughton and his friends had discussed me furtively at dinner. The dim possibility of its being a hoax stole gratefully into my unhappy mind, and once there, one's pluck came creeping back along a thousand tiny veins. My first sensation was one of blind unreasoning thankfulness that my brain was going to stand the trial. I am not a timid man, but the best of us needs some human handle to steady him in time to extremity, and in this faint but growing hope that after all it might be only a brutal hoax, I found the fulcrum that I needed. At last I moved.

'How I managed to do it I cannot tell you, but with one spring towards the foot of the bed I got within arm's-length and struck out one fearful blow with my fist at the thing. It crumbled under it, and my hand was cut to the bone. With a sickening revulsion after my terror, I dropped half-fainting across the end of the bed. So it was merely a foul trick after all. No doubt the trick had been played many a time before: no doubt Broughton and his friends had had some large bet among themselves as to what I should do when I discovered the gruesome thing. From my state of abject terror I found myself transported into an insensate anger. I shouted curses upon Broughton. I dived rather than climbed over the bed-end on to the sofa. I tore at the robed skeleton—how well the whole thing had been carried out, I thought—I broke the skull against the floor, and stamped upon its dry bones. I flung the head away under the bed, and rent the brittle bones of the trunk in pieces. I snapped the thin thigh-bones across my knee, and flung them in different directions. The shin-bones I set up against a stool and broke with my heel. I raged like a Berserker against the loathly thing, and stripped the ribs from the backbone and slung the breastbone against the cupboard. My fury increased as the work of destruction went on. I tore the frail rotten veil into twenty pieces, and the dust went up over everything, over the clean blotting-paper and the silver inkstand. At last my work was done. There was but a raffle of broken bones and strips of parchment and crumbling wool. Then, picking up a piece of the skull—it was the cheek and temple bone of the right side, I remember I opened the door and went down the passage to Broughton's dressing-room. I remember still how my sweat-dripping pyjamas clung to me as I walked. At the door I kicked and entered.

'Broughton was in bed. He had already turned the light on and seemed shrunken and horrified. For a moment he could hardly pull himself together. Then I spoke. I don't know what I said. Only I know that from a heart full and over-full with hatred and contempt, spurred on by shame of my own recent cowardice, I let my tongue run on. He answered nothing. I was amazed at my own fluency. My hair still clung lankily to my wet temples, my hand was bleeding profusely, and I must have looked a strange sight. Broughton huddled himself up at the head of the bed just as I had. Still he made no answer, no answer, no defence. He seemed pre-occupied with something besides my reproaches, and once or twice moistened his lips with his tongue. But he could say nothing though he moved his hands now and then, just as a baby who cannot speak moves its hands.

'At last the door into Mrs Broughton's room opened and she came in, white and terrified. 'What is it? What is it? Oh, in God's name! What is it?' she cried again and again, and then she went up to her husband and sat on the bed in her night-dress, and the two faced me. I told her what the matter was. I spared her husband not a word for her presence there. Yet, he seemed hardly to understand. I told the pair that I had spoiled their cowardly joke for them. Broughton looked up.

'I have smashed the foul thing into a hundred pieces,' I said. Broughton licked his lips again and his mouth worked. 'By God!' I shouted, 'it would serve you right if thrashed you within an inch of your life. I will take care that not a decent man or woman of my acquaintance ever speaks to you again. And there,' I added, throwing the broken piece of the skull upon the floor beside his bed, 'there is a souvenir for you, of your damned work tonight!'

'Broughton saw the bone, and in a moment it was his turn to frighten me. He squealed like a hare caught in a trap. He screamed and screamed till Mrs Broughton, almost as bewildered as myself, held on to him and coaxed him like a child to be quiet. But Broughton—and as he moved I thought that ten minutes ago I perhaps looked as terribly ill as he did—thrust her from him, and scrambled out of the bed on to the floor, and still screaming put out his hand to the bone. It had blood on it from my hand. He paid no attention to me whatever. In truth I said nothing. This was a new turn indeed to the horrors of the evening. He rose from the floor with the bone in his hand and stood silent. He seemed to be listening. 'Time, time, perhaps,' he muttered, and almost at the same moment fell at full length on the carpet, cutting his head against the fender. The bone flew from his hand and came to rest near the door. I picked Broughton up, haggard and broken, with blood over face. He whispered hoarsely and quickly, 'Listen, listen!' We listened.

'After ten seconds' utter quiet, I seemed to hear something.

I could not be sure, but at last there was no doubt. There was a quiet sound as of one moving along the passage. Little regular steps came towards us over the hard oak flooring. Broughton moved to where his wife sat, white and speechless, on the bed, and pressed her face into his shoulder.

'Then, the last thing that I could see as he turned the light out, he fell forward with his own head pressed into the pillow of the bed. Something in their company, something in their cowardice, helped me, and I faced the open doorway of the room, which was outlined fairly clearly against the dimly lighted passage. I put out one hand and touched Mrs Broughton's shoulder in the darkness. But at the last moment I too failed. I sank on my knees and put my face in the bed. Only we all heard. The footsteps came to the door, and there they stopped. The piece of bone was lying a yard inside the door. There was a rustle of moving stuff, and the thing was in the room. Mrs Broughton was silent: I could hear Broughton's voice praying, muffled in the pillow: I was cursing my own cowardice. Then the steps moved out again on the oak boards of the passage, and I heard the sounds dying away. In a flash of remorse I went to the door and looked out. At the end of the corridor I thought I saw something that moved away. A moment later the passage was empty. I stood with my forehead against the jamb of the door almost physically sick.

'You can turn the light on,' I said, and there was an answering flare. There was no bone at my feet. Mrs Broughton had fainted. Broughton was almost useless, and it took me ten minutes to bring her to. Broughton only said one thing worth remembering. For the most part he went on muttering prayers. But I was glad afterwards to recollect that he had said that thing. He said in a colourless voice, half as a question, half as a reproach, 'You didn't speak to her.'

'We spent the remainder of the night together. Mrs Broughton actually fell off into a kind of sleep before dawn, but she suffered so horribly in her dreams that I shook her into consciousness again. Never was dawn so long in coming. Three or four times Broughton spoke to himself. Mrs Broughton would then just tighten her hold on his arm, but she could say nothing. As for me, I can honestly say that I grew worse as the hours passed and the light strengthened. The two violent reactions had battered down my steadiness of view, and I felt that the foundations of my life had been built upon the sand. I said nothing, and after binding up my hand with a towel, I did not move. It was better so. They helped me and I helped them, and we all three knew that our reason had gone very near to ruin that night. At last, when the light came in pretty strongly, and the birds outside were chattering and singing, we felt that we must do something. Yet we never moved. You might have thought that we should particularly dislike being found as we were by the servants: yet nothing of that kind mattered a straw, and an overpowering listlessness bound us as we sat, until Chapman, Broughton's man, actually knocked and opened the door. None of us moved. Broughton, speaking hardly and stiffly, said, 'Chapman, you can come back in five minutes.' Chapman, was a discreet man, but it would have made no difference to us if he had carried his news to the 'room' at once.

'We looked at each other and I said I must go back. I meant to wait outside till Chapman returned. I simply dared not re-enter my bedroom alone. Broughton roused himself and said that he would come with me. Mrs Broughton agreed to remain in her own room for five minutes if the blinds were drawn up and all the doors left open.

'So Broughton and I, leaning stiffly one against the other, went down to my room. By the morning light that filtered past the blinds we could see our way, and I released the blinds. There was nothing wrong in the room from end to end, except smears of my own blood at the end of the bed, on the sofa, and on the carpet where I had torn the thing to pieces.'

Colvin had finished his story. There was nothing to say. Seven bells stuttered out from the fo'c'sle, and the answering cry wailed through the darkness. I took him downstairs.

'Of course, I am much better now, but it is a kindness of you to let me sleep in your cabin.'

THE THING IN THE UPPER ROOM

Arthur Morrison

A shadow hung ever over the door, which stood black in the depth of its arched recess, like an unfathomable eye under a frowning brow. The landing was wide and panelled, and a heavy rail, supported by a carved balustrade, stretched away in alternate slopes and levels down the dark staircase, past other doors, and so to the courtyard and the street. The other doors were dark also; but it was with a difference. That top landing was lightest of all, because of the skylight; and perhaps it was largely by reason of contrast that its one doorway gloomed so black and forbidding. The doors below opened and shut, slammed, stood ajar. Men and women passed in and out, with talk and human sounds—sometimes even with laughter or a snatch of song; but the door on the top landing remained shut and silent through weeks and months. For, in truth, the logement had an ill name, and had been untenanted for years. Long even before the last tenant had occupied it, the room had been regarded with fear and aversion, and the end of that last tenant had in no way lightened the gloom that hung about the place.

The house was so old that its weather-washed face may

well have looked down on the bloodshed of St. Bartholomew's, and the haunted room may even have earned its ill name on that same day of death. But Paris is a city of cruel history, and since the old mansion rose proud and new, the hotel of some powerful noble, almost any year of the centuries might have seen the blot fall on that upper room that had left it a place of loathing and shadows. The occasion was long forgotten, but the fact remained; whether or not some horror of the ancient régime or some enormity of the terror was enacted in that room was no longer to be discovered; but nobody would live there, not stay beyond that gloomy door one second longer than he could help. It might be supposed that the fate of the solitary tenant within living memory had something to do with the matter—and, indeed, his end was sinister enough; but 'long before his time the room had stood shunned and empty. He, greatly daring; had taken no more heed of the common terror of the room than to use it to his advantage in abating the rent; and he had shot himself a little later, while the police were beating at his door to arrest him on a charge of murder. As I have said, his fate may have added to the general aversion from the place, though it had in 'no way originated it; and now ten years had passed, and more, since his few articles of furniture had been carried away and sold; and nothing had been carried in to replace them.

When one is twenty-five, healthy, hungry and poor, one is less likely to be frightened from a cheap lodging by mere headshakings than might be expected in other circumstances. Attwater was twenty-five, commonly healthy, often hungry, and always poor. He came to live in Paris because, from his remembrance of his student days, he believed he could live cheaper there than in London; while it was quite certain that he would not sell fewer pictures, since he had never yet sold one.

It was the concierge of a neighbouring house who showed Attwater the room. The house of the room itself maintained no such functionary, though its main door stood open day and night. The man said little, but his surprise at Attwater's application was plain to see. Monsieur was English? Yes. The logement was convenient, though high, and probably now a little dirty, since it had not been occupied recently. Plainly, the man felt it to be no business of his to enlighten an unsuspecting foreigner as to the reputation of the place; and if he could let it there would be some small gratification from the landlord, though, at such a rent, of course a very small one indeed.

But Attwater was better informed than the concierge supposed. He had heard the tale of the haunted room, vaguely and incoherently, it is true, from the little old engraver of watches on the floor below, by whom he had been directed to the concierge. The old man had been voluble and friendly, and reported that the room had a good light, facing north-east—indeed, a much better light than he, engraver of watches, enjoyed on the floor below. So much so that, considering this advantage and the much lower rent, he himself would have taken the room long ago, except—well, except for other things. Monsieur was a stranger, and perhaps had no fear to inhabit a haunted chamber; but that was its reputation, as everybody in the quarter knew; it would be a misfortune, however, to a stranger to take the room without suspicion, and to undergo unexpected experiences. Here, however, the old man checked himself, possibly reflecting that too much information to inquirers after the upper room might offend his landlord. He hinted as much, in fact, hoping that his friendly warning would not be allowed to travel farther. As to the precise nature of the disagreeable manifestations in the room, who could say? Perhaps there were really none at all. People said this and that. Certainly, the place had been untenanted for many years, and he would not like to stay in it himself. But it might be the good fortune of monsieur to break the spell, and if monsieur was resolved to defy the *revenant,* he wished monsieur the highest success and happiness.

So much for the engraver of watches; and now the concierge of the neighbouring house led the way up the stately old panelled staircase, swinging his keys in his hand, and halted at last before the dark door in the frowning recess. He turned the key with some difficulty, pushed open the door, and stood back with an action of something not wholly deference, to allow Attwatet to enter first.

A sort of small lobby had been partitioned off at some time, though except for this the logement was of one large room only. There was something unpleasant in the air of the place—not a smell, when one came to analyse one's sensations, though at first it might seem so. Attwater walked across to the wide window and threw it open. The chimneys and roofs of many houses of all ages straggled before him, and out of the welter rose the twin towers of St. Sulpice, scarred and grim.

Air the room as one might, it was unpleasant; a sickly, even a cowed, feeling, invaded one through all the senses—or perhaps through none of them. The feeling was there, though it was not easy to say by what channel it penetrated. Attwater was resolved to admit none but a common-sense explanation, and blamed the long closing of door and window; and the concierge, standing uneasily near the door, agreed that that must be it. For a moment Attwater wavered, despite himself. But the rent was very low, and, low as it was, he could not afford a sou more.

The light was good, though it was not a top-light, and the place was big enough for his simple requirements. Attwater reflected that he should despise himself ever after if he shrank from the opportunity; it would be one of those secret humiliations that will rise again and again in a man's memory, and make him blush in solitude. He told the concierge to leave door and window wide open for the rest of the day, and he clinched the bargain.

It was with something of amused bravado that he reported to his few friends in Paris his acquisition of a haunted room; for, once out of the place, he readily convinced himself that his disgust and dislike while in the room were the result of imagination and nothing more. Certainly, there was no rational reason to account for the unpleasantness; consequently, what could it be but a matter of fancy? He resolved to face the matter from the beginning, and clear his mind from any foolish prejudices that the hints of the old engraver might have inspired, by forcing himself through whatever adventures he might encounter. In fact, as he walked the streets about his business, and arranged for the purchase and delivery of the few simple articles of furniture that would be necessary, his enterprise assumed the guise of a pleasing adventure. He remembered that he had made an attempt, only a year or two ago, to spend a night in a house reputed haunted in England, but had failed to find the landlord. Here was the adventure to hand, with promise of a tale to tell in future times; and a welcome idea struck him that he might look out the ancient history of the room, and work the whole thing into a magazine article, which would bring a little money.

So simple were his needs that by the afternoon of the day following his first examination of the room it was ready for use. He took his bag from the cheap hotel in a little street of

Montparnasse, where he had been lodging, and carried it to his new home. The key was now in his pocket, and for the first time he entered the place alone.' The window remained wide open; but it was still there—that depressing, choking something that entered the consciousness he knew not by what gate. Again he accused his fancy. He stamped and whistled, and set about unpacking a few canvases and a case of old oriental weapons that were part of his professional properties. But he could give no proper attention to the work, and detected himself more than once yielding to a childish impulse to look over his shoulder. He laughed at himself—with some effort—and sat determinedly to smoke a pipe, and grow used to his surroundings. But presently he found himself, pushing his chair farther and farther back, till it touched the wall. He would take the whole room into view, he said to himself in excuse, and stare-it out of countenance. So he sat and smoked, and as he sat his eye fell on a Malay dagger that lay on the table between him and the window. It was a murderous, twisted thing, and its pommel was fashioned into the semblance of a bird's head, with curved beak and an eye of some dull red stone. He found himself gazing, on this red eye with an odd, mindless fascination. The dagger in its wicked curves seemed now a creature of some outlandish fantasy—a snake with a beaked head, a thing of nightmare, in some new way dominant, overruling the centre of his perceptions. The rest of the room grew dim, but the red stone glowed with a fuller light; nothing more was present to his consciousness, Then, with a sudden clang, the heavy bell of St. Sulpice aroused him, and he started up in some surprise.

There lay the dagger on the table, strange and murderous enough, but merely as he had always known, it. Her observed with more surprise, however, that his chair, which had been back against the wall, was now some six feet forward, close by the table; clearly, he must have drawn it forward in his abstraction, towards, the dagger on which his eyes had been fixed... The great bell of St. Sulpice went clanging on, repeating its monotonous call to the Angelus.

He was cold, almost shivering. He flung the dagger into a drawer, and turned to go out. He saw by his watch that it was later than he had supposed; his fit of abstraction must have lasted some time. Perhaps he had even been dozing.

He went slowly downstairs and out into the streets. As he went he grew more and more ashamed of himself, for he had to confess that in some inexplicable way he feared that room. He had seen nothing, heard nothing of the kind that one might have expected, or had heard of in any room reputed haunted; he could not help thinking that it would have been some sort of relief if he had. But there was an all-pervading, overpowering sense of another Presence—something abhorrent, not human, something almost physically nauseous. Withal it was something more than presence; it was power, domination—so he seemed to remember it. And yet the remembrance grew weaker as he walked in the gathering dusk; he thought of a story he had once read of a haunted house wherein it was shown that the house actually was haunted—by the spirit of fear, and nothing else. That, he persuaded himself, was the case with his room; he felt angry at the growing conviction that he had allowed himself to be overborne by fancy—by the spirit of fear.

He returned that night with the resolve to allow himself no foolish indulgence. He had heard nothing and had seen nothing; when something palpable to the senses occurred, it would be time enough to deal with it. He took off his clothes and got into bed deliberately, leaving candle and matches at hand in case of need. He had expected to find some difficulty in sleeping, or at least some delay, but he was scarce well in bed ere he fell into a heavy sleep.

Dazzling sunlight through the window woke him in the morning, and he sat up, staring sleepily about him. He must have slept like a log. But he had been dreaming; the dreams were horrible. His head ached beyond anything he had experienced before, and he was far more tired than when he went to bed. He sank back on the pillow, but the mere contact made his head ring with pain. He got out of bed, and found himself staggering; it was all as though he had been drunk-unspeakably drunk with bad liquor. His dreams—they had been horrid dreams; he could remember that they had been bad; but what they actually were was now gone from him entirely. He rubbed his eyes and stared amazedly down at the table: where the crooked dagger lay, with its bird's head and red stone eye. It lay just as it had lain when he sat gazing at it yesterday, and yet he would have sworn that he had flung that same dagger into a drawer. Perhaps he had dreamed it; at any rate, he put the thing carefully into the drawer now; and, still with his ringing headache, dressed himself and went out.

As he reached the next landing the old engraver greeted him from his door with an inquiring good-day. 'Monsieur has not slept well, I fear?'

In some doubt, Attwater protested that he had slept quite soundly, 'And as yet I have neither seen nor heard anything of the ghost,' he added.

'Nothing?' replied the old man, with a lift of the eyebrows, 'nothing at all? It is fortunate. It seemed to me, here below, that monsieur was moving about very restlessly in the night; but no doubt I was mistaken. No doubt, also, I may felicitate monsieur on breaking the evil tradition. We shall hear no more of it; monsieur has the good fortune of a brave heart.'

He smiled and bowed pleasantly, but it was with something of a puzzled look that his eyes followed Attwater descending the staircase.

Attwater took his coffee and roll after an hour's walk, and fell asleep in his seat. Not for long, however, and presently he rose and left the cafe. He felt better, though still unaccountably fatigued. He caught sight of his face in a mirror beside a shop window, and saw an improvement since he had looked in his own glass. That indeed had brought him a shock. Worn and drawn beyond what might have been expected of so bad a night, there was even something more. What was it? How should it remind him of that old legend—was it Japanese?—which he had tried to recollect when he had wondered confusedly at the haggard apparition that confronted him? Some tale of a demon-possessed person who in any mirror, saw never his own face, but the face of the demon.

Work he felt to be impossible, and he spent the day on garden seats, at café tables, and for a while in the Luxembourg. And in the evening he met an English friend, who took him by the shoulders and looked into his eyes, shook him, and declared that he had been overworking, and needed, above all things, a good dinner, which he should have instantly. 'You'll dine with me,' he said, 'at La Perouse, and we'll get a cab to take us there. I'm hungry.'

As they stood and looked for a passing cab a man ran shouting with newspapers. 'We'll have a cab,' Attwater's friend repeated, 'and we'll take the new murder with us for conversation's sake. Hi! *Journal!*'

He bought a paper, and followed Attwater into the cab.

'I've a strong idea I knew the poor old boy by sight,' he said. 'I believe he'd seen better days.'

'Who?'

'The old man who was murdered in the Rue Broca last night. The description fits exactly. He used to hang about the cafés and run messages. It isn't easy to read in this cab; but there's probably nothing fresh in this edition. They haven't caught the murderer, anyhow.'

Attwater took the paper, and struggled to read it in the changing light. A poor old man had been found dead on the footpath of the Rue Broca, torn with a score of stabs. He had been identified—an old man not known to have a friend in the world; also, because he was so old and so poor, probably not an enemy. There was no robbery; the few sous the old man possessed remained in his pocket. He must have been attacked on his way home in the early hours of the morning, possibly by a homicidal maniac, and stabbed again and again with inconceivable fury. No arrest had been made.

Attwater pushed the paper away: 'Pah!' he said; 'I don't like it. I'm a bit off colour and I was dreaming horribly all last night; thought why this should remind me of it I can't guess. But it's no cure for the blues, this!'

'No,' replied his friend heartily; 'We'll get that upstairs, for here we are, on the quay. A bottle of the best Burgundy on the list and the best dinner they can do—that's your physic. Come!'

It was a good prescription, indeed. Attwater's friend was cheerful and assiduous, and nothing could have bettered the dinner. Attwater found himself reflecting that indulgence in the blues was a poor pastime, with no better excuse than a bad night's rest. And last night's dinner in comparison with this! Well, it was enough to have spoiled his sleep, that one franc-fifty dinner.

Attwater left La Perouse as gay as his friend. They had sat late, and now there was nothing to do but cross the water and walk a little in the boulevards. This they did, and finished the evening at a café table with half a dozen acquaintances.

Attwater walked home with a light step, feeling less drowsy than at any time during the day. He was well enough. He felt he should soon get used to the room. He had been a little too much alone lately, and that had got on his nerves. It was simply stupid.

Again he slept quickly and heavily—and dreamed. But he had an awakening of another sort. No bright sun blazed in at the open window to lift his heavy lids, and no morning bell from St. Sulpice opened his ears to the cheerful noise of the city. He awoke gasping and staring in the dark, rolling face-downward on the floor, catching his breath in agonized sobs; while through the window from the streets came a clamour of hoarse cries: cries of pursuit and the noise of running men: a shouting and clatter wherein here and there a voice was clear among the rest—*Al'assassin! Arrêtez!*'

He dragged himself to his feet in the dark, gasping still. What was this—all this? Again a dream? His legs trembled under him, and he sweated with fear. He made for the window, panting and feeble; and then, as he supported himself by the sill, he realized wonderingly that he was fully dressed that he wore even his hat. The running crowd straggled through the outer street and away, the shouts growing fainter. What had wakened him? Why had he dressed? He remembered his matches, and turned to grope for them; but something was already in his hand—something wet, sticky. He dropped it on the table, and even as he struck the light, before he saw it, he knew. The match sputtered and flared, and there on the table lay the crooked dagger, smeared and dripping and horrible.

Blood was on his hands—the match stuck in his fingers. Caught at the heart by the first grip of an awful surmise, he hooked up and saw in the mirror before him, in the last flare of the match, the face of the Thing in the room.